# The Dingbatter Case

## A Tucker Crime Novel

Written by Larry F. Hunter

# The Dingbatter Case: A Tucker Crime Novel

**The Tucker Crime Novels, Volume 2**

Larry Hunter

Published by Larry Hunter, 2013.

The Dingbatter Case: A Tucker Crime Novel



By Larry F. Hunter

This is a work of fiction. Similarities to real people, places, or events are entirely coincidental.

THE DINGBATTER CASE: A TUCKER CRIME NOVEL

**First edition. July 20, 2013.**



ISBN: 979-8227884398

Written by Larry Hunter.

ISBN 9798227884398

The Dingbatter Case

A Tucker Crime Novel

Published by Larry Hunter

# Dedication

This Novel is dedicated to my lovely wife, love of my life, without whose

encouragement and help it would never have been completed.

# Chapter 1 Arrival

Tucker sat comfortably in the soft leather passenger seat of the big Winnebago RV and watched Susan maneuver through the congestion in Morehead City, North Carolina, as they headed toward an Emerald Isle RV park to spend a few weeks catching some sun and doing a little fishing. In the months since they'd met, during the National Park murder case, they'd been inseparable and while marriage had occurred to them both individually, they hadn't discussed it. Being in their early fifties, with no real attachments, there was no hurry. Tucker turned to admire Susan, watching her petite form, as she handled the RV like a pro, seeming totally at ease, driving the long vehicle in the traffic that was always a feature of the beach areas during early fall. The weather had been cool of late and this meant that the days would be good for fishing and the nights good for, well, night stuff. Susan glanced in his direction and said, "What are you looking at Tucker, never seen a woman drive a big rig before?"

Tucker's response indicated his feelings, "Never one as beautiful as you." He continued, making small talk, "How long do you think until we get to the park? I'm sure glad we waited until after the hurricane to come down. Based on all the junk in the road, it must have been a mess down here."

There'd been a pretty big storm that had hit the outer banks and with the winds and large amounts of rainfall the area looked pretty torn up. It was obvious that there had been some flooding here as well. They'd been headed south from near the Great Lakes when the hurricane hit the news and they'd stayed in the mountains of Virginia for a few days waiting for the storm to subside before continuing to the North Carolina coast, missing the bulk of the weather in doing so. October hurricanes were frequent in this part of the world and Tucker hoped this recent storm would be the last of the season so their visit could be peaceful.

Being a North Carolina native, Tucker knew the beauty of the NC lower banks islands. He really wanted to spend some time here and let Susan see the stark contrast between the local scenery and the California coast she was familiar with. When he'd been a cop in Salisbury, Tucker had spent a fair amount of time here, mostly fishing off Davis Island in the surf, but with the occasional Beaufort deep sea excursion. He'd fallen in love with the area and the quirky locals, particularly the residents of Harkers Island.

Tucker said, "You'll like all the local area but the most unique is Harkers Island. It was separated from the rest of the State until the 1800's when the only bridge was built and has a different culture and people. There aren't many folks living there, mostly fishermen whose families have been on the island for generations. I spent a lot of time on the island in my previous life and got to know several of the locals and I'll tell you, they're a trip. Not in a bad way, just very different from anyone you've ever met before. Makes you think of the mountain clans in the way they live and work together."

He wanted Susan to enjoy his old haunting grounds and the oddities of the people as much as he had. He sat and reminisced about the past as Susan headed them toward their destination, the campground at Emerald Isle.

Susan said, "We're getting close. It looks like there's a Wal Mart Center just ahead. Should we stop and stock up before going to the campground? It might save us a trip back here, if the parking lot's empty enough for us to get in."

Tucker replied, "Sounds good. Let's check it out."

While they would normally set up in a campground and take Tucker's pickup, which they towed behind the Winnebago, Tucker was anxious to get to the beach and check out the surf, so this seemed like a good idea. He could pick up some local newspapers as well. The lot was open so they turned into the Wal Mart and parked out near the road, hoping no one would block them in. They walked toward the front door hand in hand.

About a half hour later they were headed back toward the RV pushing two baskets of supplies when Tucker said, "Did you notice the clerk's accent? That's one of the unique things down here I was telling you about. They call that the "Carolina Brogue". It's the way the local folks, High Tiders or Hoi Toiders in their brogue, talk and for years it drove me nuts trying to understand. I still have some difficulty, but I think it sounds pretty cool now."

Susan replied, "I thought maybe she was a foreigner or something. I could only catch a word now and then; interesting though."

They entered the RV and as Susan drove out of the lot, Tucker began to read the local Morehead City and Beaufort newspapers. It was nearly dark by the time they'd checked into the campground and finished all the necessary set up. When everything was in place both Tucker and Susan were bone tired and retired for the night to get some rest. It had been a long day, and they were both ready for some quiet rest time here on the beach.

It was nearly seven when Tucker woke up, easing out of bed so as not to disturb Susan, as she slept on. He quietly closed the bedroom door and made coffee before exiting the RV and sitting down to enjoy the ocean view, the smells, and the sounds emanating from the beach. The previous evening, when he'd read the Beaufort Observer, he'd seen that in the aftermath of the hurricane a body had washed up on Shackleford Banks and, being the old cop he was, his curiosity was aroused. He read the article again and then looked for more information in the Morehead City newspaper.

The body of an adult male approximately fifty years old had been found near the beach on Shackleford Banks after the hurricane. It was discovered when several of the indigenous wild horses were observed standing on the beach and a fisherman, when attempting to get closer to see the horses, had stumbled on the remains. The local medical examiner was still working to determine the cause of death and to identify the body, as there'd been no wallet or anything else to identify the person.

Tucker knew this could be nothing but a victim of the hurricane who had drowned while attempting to get off the island, but he had a gut feeling this was not the case. While none of his business, he still had enough cop in him that curiosity and the desire to investigate, would prevent him just ignoring this case, particularly with his long term connection with the local area. After all, he might know the victim. He decided if this was more than a natural death, he would at least contact the local authorities and volunteer to help. He figured neither the local city nor Carteret County authorities had much experience investigating murders so he might be able to help, if that's what this turned out to be. With just a little excitement, he went back to drinking his coffee and waiting for Susan to rouse.

Susan awakened in a wonderful mood when she realized where they were. A few weeks in coastal North Carolina seemed just what the doctor ordered. She and Tucker had just left upstate New York in the nick of time as the weather there had started to turn colder, and the lake breezes were getting stronger and damper as each day passed. While they truly enjoyed the majesty of the trees and the falling leaves, it had been time to escape to the moderate weather of the mid-south. When Tucker had reminisced about the times he'd visited the lower banks, she'd thought it might be just the thing to help him relax and let the two of them explore this relationship of theirs. She believed he still had reservations based on her behavior when they had met and the situation that had brought them together. She truly regretted her behavior in that incident but felt they both needed to move on. She was, after all, a grown woman. She had not been at her best and was actively making it up to Tucker as they spent more time together. Susan truly enjoyed the RV lifestyle and being with Tucker just completed the deal and she felt together they could have a very good life traveling and mostly doing nothing. She hoped he felt the same.

Susan went into the kitchen to the smell of brewed coffee. Glancing outside she saw Tucker sitting in the lounge chair, reading the newspaper he'd picked up the previous day. She opened the RV door and asked, "More coffee?" and Tucker responded by getting up and handing her his empty thermal cup. He smiled openly and pulled her down from the steps planting a heartfelt kiss on her lips. It was as if he had felt her insecurity and was communicating that everything was well. They both felt the warmth only sincere love can bring and in that moment, as they looked into each other's eyes, both were aware of a new commitment and peace in their relationship. Susan broke away and re-entering the RV went to get them both a cup of coffee. Returning outside, she sat beside Tucker and looked at his discarded paper immediately noticing the article about the body that had washed up on the island. She sipped her coffee and said quietly.

"Even here in this peaceful area there are murders. Do you miss being a cop, Tucker?" To which he replied, "This is probably not a murder and besides, I've got you so my life is pretty full, but yeah, I miss the investigation thing just a bit."

"After we have our nice peaceful vacation here maybe you might like to become a Private Detective. I've always thought they were sexy. Remember Magnum on TV?" She said somewhat jokingly.

Tucker had to think a bit to come up with a response. "PI's mostly do divorce, finding folks, that kind of thing. The real interesting investigating for murders, serial killers, rapists and such is done by the police because most people can't afford to hire a PI for that kind of thing."

Susan's response surprised Tucker. "Maybe you could help folks for free or as the lawyers call it, pro bono, or something like that. We don't really need any money and if it would make you happy, I'm for it."

Tucker thought to himself; What a wonderful woman I've found! He actually believed that she wouldn't object to a hobby of investigating. He said, "What would you do while I'm out solving the crime of the century? You'd be awful bored sitting around this camper waiting for me."

"Do you remember Hart to Hart on TV? Robert Wagner was sexy too and I can be Stephanie Powers!" Susan exclaimed.

Tucker reached for her and looking into her beautiful brown eyes he said, "You're too pretty to be Stephanie Powers." then he leaned forward to kiss her again.

"Let's go to Harkers Island for breakfast. It'll take about an hour or so but there's a little grill in the gas station that serves a good meal, if it's still there, and I can show you some of the sites on the island while we're there. We can stop in Morehead City on the way back and do a little shopping, if you like."

Susan nodded and went inside to get ready, leaving Tucker to contemplate becoming an amateur PI as a hobby. Fishing can only occupy so much time, he thought, smiling. He wondered what it would take to get a license since he'd been a cop already. His smile broadened into a grin as he took another sip of coffee.

# Chapter 2 First Visit to the Island

Susan was intrigued by the stark contrast in the living styles that the houses demonstrated as they drove through the little town of Beaufort toward Harkers Island. There were million-dollar homes surrounded by dwellings that could only be described as shacks, abandoned cars, broken fences, and other signs of neglect, visible all around. While aware of the disparity in incomes that existed in these areas with the natives supporting themselves by fishing or tourist services and the big money represented by newcomers whose wealth was made elsewhere, she had a hard time when confronted with the difference face to face. Her own past marriage, to a now imprisoned accountant, had left her quite well off but she was amazed at the huge homes that were obviously unoccupied most of the year and represented summer homes for the rich and famous here. In California the same situation existed but was not as harshly visible. They went past a sign indicating the town limit of Bettie where it looked as if time had stopped in the 1950's and she could only wonder why the locals remained here at the mercy of the considerable storms and flooding but then realized that much of what looked like a very rundown town was simply the remains of the devastation caused by the recent hurricane. She supposed that in another season, absent hurricanes, this would be quite a beautiful area and with the Pamlico Sound and the ocean so close, life could be very good here.

Tucker was driving as they approached the bridge over the Sound that was the only access to Harkers Island. The bridge was turned to allow a boat to pass and as they sat waiting, he pointed out the landmarks on either side of the bridge, telling Susan that over the two decades he'd visited the island the population had increased tremendously with most of the growth being newcomers called "Dingbatters" by the locals. He went on to explain this meant non-natives who visited the island or came to live there. This amused Susan. She was laughing as the bridge turned and they moved forward and shortly turned into the parking lot of the gas station which was also an eating establishment. They entered, hand in hand, sitting at one of the empty booths and were soon approached by a young waitress who asked in her brogue, "Can I help you?"

Tucker said, "Two coffees and menus, please".

The young lady pointed at a chalkboard on the wall, smiled and went to get their coffee. In just a few moments she returned and placed cups in front of them, pouring steaming black coffee for each. She turned, as a young man obviously a local based on his accent said, "Becky, I need some more coffee and mustard for my ham biscuit."

Susan leaned over to Tucker and whispered quietly, "You don't hear that much in California!" and then chuckled. She looked around the room noticing the pictures of fishermen with their catches, the tackle, rods and other paraphernalia associated with island life and thought it was quaint but homey in the restaurant. She liked it.

They sat, sipping coffee and soon Tucker got up and went outside to pick up the day's newspaper. Returning and looking at the first page, he saw in big block letters above the fold on page one, 'Murder on Shackleford Banks' and began to read the accompanying article. When he finished, he raised his head and summarized the news for Susan.

"The body found was not just a drowning. The man was beaten badly, almost to the point of torture, and apparently left to die on the island. Using fingerprints, they've identified who it is but all they'll say is it's not a local until the next of kin is notified. They have no idea how he got on the island since the only way is by boat and there were no boats found. A good guess is that someone took him out there, killed him there and came back to the mainland on the boat. Even here in this rural area folks get murdered."

Susan took the newspaper from Tucker's hand and scanned the article herself as Tucker continued to speak.

"It was probably a property owner that got killed while down here to check on things after the hurricane. The family might not even have noticed he was missing, if he was down here alone, and they're just waiting at home for him to call and report on the condition of their house down here. Of course, it could be a transient or someone just visiting in Beaufort. I guess we'll know soon enough."

On the other side of the restaurant, Tucker became aware of a conversation, in a group of what were obviously locals, concerning the body that had been found. He heard several comments that included, "Glad it wasn't one of us."

"Musta been a Dingbatter"

"This kinda thing didn't used to happen here."

"It's getting like the city down here."

Tucker sympathized with them and wished for older more peaceful times himself. He then turned his attention to a table of older women sitting in the center of the room. These ladies were not locals, indicated by their dress, and they were conversing in low tones making it hard for him to hear, but loud enough to confirm their status as Dingbatters. He heard one of them say, "I hope it wasn't Stella's husband. They haven't been down this year like they normally are, but I did see someone near their house last weekend.

It's not that far to New Bern. I've been a little concerned that they haven't been down this summer or this fall. I've been meaning to call but I just couldn't now, with the murder and all."

Susan interrupted his eavesdropping with a comment, "I wonder how long ago the man was killed? They don't say in this article. This could have happened before the hurricane and the body was exposed by the high water and wind. Maybe that bit of information will be released tomorrow."

"Are you beginning to think like a detective, dear?" Tucker asked in a humorous tone. "Mrs. Hart is on the case."

They both chuckled quietly so as not to seem irreverent to the crowd. About then their breakfast arrived and they started to eat, both of them continuing to listen stealthily to the conversations around them for other insight into the murder.

After some time, Tucker said to Susan, "When we leave here, let's take a little drive around the island and maybe do a little shopping at the grocery store here. The prices are higher than on the mainland, but I want to see if the older guy who used to work there is still around. Haven't seen him in several years and he might not remember me but he should. Is that OK?"

"Of course, baby! We're in no hurry and I'd like to see the island and meet some of your old friends as well."

"Not really friends but acquaintances. You have to live here for years before anyone would become a friend. On the positive side, once you are accepted you become a part of the island and everyone knows you."

They finished their meal and after Tucker left cash to cover the check as well as a generous tip, they exited and got into his pickup to start the island tour. Susan looked around curiously as they drove over the island, saying little as Tucker described the changes that had occurred since his last visit. The old motel was gone, several waterfront homes he remembered had been replaced with huge mansions that blocked the water view for everyone around them, docks extended far out into the sound blocking what used to be oyster beds and good fishing areas, huge boats, some practically yachts, floated where small slips accommodating several fishing boats used to be. The island appeared to have been invaded by money. He felt some sadness at that. Modern America was rapidly overtaking this little spot changing it forever, and in his opinion not for the better. As he described all this, Susan listened raptly and issued the occasional comment in agreement. At last they turned into "Bob's", the local grocery, hardware, and fishing tackle store. Entering the glass front doors, Tucker immediately saw that not everything on the island had changed. Bob's was still the same old store. Thank goodness, he thought to himself, as he walked down the aisle with Susan to check out the fishing tackle.

Susan commented, "I love this store. It makes me think of the old store in Kansas that my parents owned. We had all this kind of stuff, and we were the only store in the small town I spent my first 9 years in. It sure takes me back."

Tucker replied, "This kind of place is on the endangered list and I really can't believe this one's still here. I guess the 1600 folks that live here on the island can't support a Food King. I wager that within 5 years Bob's is gone and there's a chain store here on the island. The locals like this place but I'm not so sure about the newcomers."

Susan replied, "It'll be missed." and they continued down each aisle selecting some items they needed before heading up front to the checkout lane. When the young lady was finished checking their choices Tucker asked, "Is Ralph still working here?" She replied, pointing, "Yeah, he's in the office down there to the right. Go on back if you want to see him."

Susan grabbed the groceries and headed out to the truck saying, "You go visit a minute; I'm just gonna look around outside. Take your time but come get me after you catch up so I can meet him."

Tucker nodded and headed toward the raised office where he saw Ralph, a little grayer and plumper, hunched over a computer screen looking somewhat frustrated. Suddenly Ralph blurted "Damn" and slid back in his seat raising his hands over his head with a grunt.

Tucker said, "What's the matter, Redneck?" hoping Ralph would remember him and not be insulted with the redneck comment. Tucker had always called him redneck since they'd first met some twenty years ago.

Ralph's face flashed angrily as he looked over at Tucker, but this immediately changed to a big grin as he recognized his friend from long ago.

"Tucker, how the hell are you? How long has it been? Heard you retired, is that true? Man, it's good to see you." This all streamed from Ralph as he came around the cubicle wall and gave Tucker a bear hug which Tucker returned vigorously.

"Ralph, it's good to see you, too. Yeah, I'm retired and just touring around in an RV seeing the countryside and enjoying life. We're staying at the campground on Emerald Isle and just came over here to eat breakfast and see you."

"We? So you're still married to what's her name?"

Tucker hesitated, then replied, "Janet, but we divorced not too long after the last time I saw you. I'm traveling with a wonderful lady I met while on the road. We've been together for about six months or so and she's just outside. I'll go get her if you have time to visit for a few minutes."

Ralph smiled and said, "I didn't really like Janet anyways so go get this new one. Knowing you, she's gonna be a treat for these old eyes and I need some cheering up after this damn inventory I'm doing."

Tucker laughed and went outside to fetch Susan, quickly returning with her in tow. Ralph gave Susan an up and down look and then winked at Tucker saying, "Yep, she's a looker all right." Susan's initial response was an embarrassed look and a demure smile as if she were unaccustomed to compliments from blunt older gentlemen.

She blushed, then smiling at Ralph, responded by turning to Tucker saying," I thought you said he was old?" They all laughed and relaxed at this.

The conversation went through the normal catching up and eventually turned to current events on the island. At this point Tucker asked Ralph, "Are you still the community watch leader here on the island? Still close to the sheriff's department?"

Ralph nodded affirmatively and said, "I thought you were retired. Still a cop on the inside, I guess."

"Well, you know, once a cop always a cop. Have you heard anything more about the body found on Shackleford Banks? We read about it in the newspaper and I was wondering if it might be anyone I knew from the old days."

"I'm still close to the sheriff but the only thing I've heard is that it's the body of a Dingbatter who was down to check on his place after the hurricane. They think the murder was somewhere else and the body was dropped on the island. Beat to death like the paper said and hurt pretty bad before he died. They asked us on the island to be on the lookout for any strangers around but you know how that is. Hell, you're a stranger after all these years."

Tucker bit his lower lip as he thought about this and then asked, "Do you know who it is, Ralph? Any chance you knew him?"

"You can bet I knew him, I know everyone here, but they wouldn't tell me yet. When I find out, I'll let you know, if you give me your cell number."

Tucker gave Ralph his number and he and Susan left, vowing to come back and visit the next time they made it to the island. As they drove back down toward the island bridge heading toward Morehead City for some shopping, they were both thinking about the murder of the island visitor and how horrible it would be for the family back on the mainland when they were notified. Expecting to hear about a second home being damaged when the police arrived and actually being told of a murder would be devastating, and they both wished they could do something to ease the hurt.

Tucker said, "When they announce who the victim is, maybe we can go visit the family and do something. Help with arrangements, offer sympathy, something."

"It's really none of our business but we have some time so maybe we could just drop by and lend an ear, particularly if it's someone you used to know."

---

They drove into Morehead City eventually finding a parking spot in spite of all the beach traffic. After strolling the streets and checking out the waterfront, it was time for lunch. They entered the next seafood place they came to, which by its name offered the very best in clean seafood, and by the size of the line to enter, made them think that the food must be good as well. They sat down and were immediately approached by a nice middle-aged server whose nametag declared that she was to be addressed as Savannah. Tucker bit his tongue to avoid commenting on her being in the wrong city, as he was sure she had heard this hundreds of times in the past and simply said, "Good afternoon, Savannah. We'd like two teas and some sweetener for me. The lady is not from around here and sweet is not her cup of tea." He chuckled at his own terrible joke and Savannah merely smiled an 'Oh, Brother' smile and went to fetch their drinks and some menus.

Tucker listened to the buzz in the room and couldn't help hearing the talk at the table just to the right. The conversation he eavesdropped on was about the body found on the island. It appeared that the identity was known by now and it had been confirmed that it was a Dingbatter who lived in New Bern, about an hour away toward the west. He strained to hear more, without seeming too nosy, but finally just slid his chair over and introduced himself and simply asked for more details. The couple talking turned out to be part time Harkers Island residents who had come over to the mainland for lunch and knew the local sheriff who'd told them that the wife had been notified and thus he could tell them as well. It turned out the murdered man was in his sixties, rather than the younger age as reported earlier. The body had been exposed for quite some time explaining the discrepancy in the age estimate. Listening closely, Tucker finally interrupted and asked the man's name.

The lady said, "Well, I suppose it's all right to tell you now since it'll be in the paper tomorrow. His name was George Stallings.

They're from New Bern. It's so sad. Stella must be just torn up. Their children are grown and gone. I believe she was originally from New York. She'll have no one to be with her down here. Poor thing."

Her husband spoke up then and said, "We need to go up there and visit with her and see if we can help."

As they rambled on, Tucker tried to place the name, and he finally concluded that he just didn't know this couple. He interrupted the couple to ask, "How long have they been here on the island?"

The man thought for a few seconds and then said, "I think they bought their place about 4 years after we got ours. Maybe 6 years ago. Yes, 6 years ago."

Tucker said, "I'm sorry I interrupted you but I just wanted to see if perhaps the man was someone I knew from a while ago when I visited Harkers quite a bit, but they came after I quit visiting down here. You guys have a pleasant afternoon and perhaps we'll see you again."

When Tucker and Susan had finished their meal they left the restaurant, strolling down the waterfront toward their vehicle looking at the fishing boats and the crowd of people walking like they were on this pleasant sunny fall day. Neither spoke for a time, both feeling sympathy for the poor woman whose life had just been turned upside down and how very lonely she must be. After a while Susan spoke.

"Tucker, we've both been on vacation for months now and I can see that while I thought you needed some time relaxing, in fact, you're probably bored. You seem more relaxed here after getting interested in this murder case than you've been since we got together. Why don't we visit Mrs. Stallings and see if there's anything we can do to help her get through this horrible time."

Tucker thought to himself, she really is the best thing that ever happened to me, and said, "Let's go by the Sheriff's Office here and see how mad it'll make them if we get involved. The last thing I want to do is irritate the local guys. And oh, I love you, you know that!"

Susan's lips turned up in a smile as she thought, yep, he just needs to be involved.

When they arrived at the county sheriff's office, the young deputy at the front desk seemed at first reluctant to let them see the sheriff, but when Tucker explained that he was a retired cop the deputy relaxed and called the sheriff to the front. A large red-faced man with a booming voice entered the room and, grabbing Tucker's hand, said, "Glad to meet you, sir. And your name is Mr. Tucker, right? I'm Sheriff Watson. What can I do for you?"

Tucker replied, "Just Tucker will be fine. Can we have just a little of your time today? We have a favor to ask of you."

"You and the little woman come on into my office. Always time for a man in blue, you know."

Tucker and Susan followed him and took seats across from the huge wooden desk that held a laptop and just a couple of folders and nothing more. Tucker resisted the urge to comment on the light workload the desk indicated, thinking better of it before his wise crack nature came forth.

"All right Tucker, what's on your mind?"

Tucker began his explanation with a brief history of himself.

"I'm a retired cop from Salisbury. Susan and I have been traveling around in a motorhome seeing the sights. We're staying on Emerald Isle at the campground and checking out the local area.

Before I retired, I used to come to Harkers Island a lot and got sorta fond of the place."

Watson interrupted, "Not to be too nosey, but you seem pretty young to be retired from the Salisbury force. Most folks with that kind of job stay as long as they can. Good Duty, I've heard."

"I was shot on a stakeout a few years back and medically retired from the force. You heard right, it's a great place to work and if I could, I'd still be there but I have a lead souvenir the shooter left me near my spine and the doctors won't clear me for duty. I'm completely healed though, and other than some occasional pain, I'm good to go."

"Did you get the guy?" asked the Sheriff.

"We know who did it but without conclusive evidence the force can't do anything. His time will come. It's still an open case."

Tucker resumed his explanation of why he and Susan were there. "When we got here we saw in the paper that there had been a body found on Shackleford. I know you guys can handle everything but with my background I thought I might be able to help you with this case since I've got a lot of time on my hands. I was a Detective first grade there in Salisbury so I know my way around a murder case. I was helping the FBI on some interstate murders when Susan and I met. Do you think that'd be OK? We won't interfere with your investigation and will share anything we find with you guys as soon as we get it. How about it?"

The Sheriff rubbed his ear and was visibly thinking about his response. Finally he said, "Our little department here don't get many murders and frankly we could use some expertise. This might go federal, and the FBI may have other thoughts but as far as I'm concerned, I'd be grateful for the help. If you've already worked with the FBI then I guess they won't mind either, if they end up taking the case. Can't pay you, of course, and if the feds say skedaddle you gotta go."

Tucker hadn't realized the island was federal property and figured that he could probably stay with the case even if it went federal by calling Andy Jessup, the agent he had worked with before on the national park thing. Jessup might actually be the agent in charge of this case, which would make Tucker's access to case information, especially forensics, even easier. He was beginning to get enthused and wanted to get the show on the road.

He said, "Sheriff Watson, we appreciate this. Between you, us, and the FBI we'll find the killer, I'm sure. Thanks, we can find our own way out." As they walked to the door, Tucker turned and asked, "Do you know what I have to do to be a licensed Private Investigator in North Carolina?"

The Sheriff smiled and said, "I think as a retired cop all you have to do is fill out some form and apply. Might need a sponsor and if that's the case, you help me solve this murder and I'll sponsor you. Good Luck!"

Tucker's step was visibly lighter as he and Susan walked back toward their pickup to head toward the campground. Susan reflected on this change in their life together and decided that being the female half of a detective team might actually be a good way to spend time together. She smiled as she followed Tucker realizing that she'd fallen for him, completely.

# Chapter 3 The Case Begins

Tucker and Susan had talked about their budding careers as PI's until the wee hours and both were excited to start the next morning. When they woke up, Tucker immediately went online to try to locate the widow of the victim using Google. Knowing both the name and the location where he had lived, it was relatively easy to gather information on the victim. Tucker read the biographical information and recited the high spots to Susan as she sat nearby.

"Stallings was President of a local bank in New Bern. He and his wife had two kids. They were active in both community activities and in their church. He was a member of the Rotary Club as well as the Civitan Club. They were apparently quite well off as his parents had left him a large farm that is still active in growing tobacco and cotton. They bought their beach house about six years ago. They'd already bought two other small homes on the island that they leased to summer visitors. All in all, a pretty normal upper-class life with nothing to indicate why anyone would want to kill him."

Susan said, "Most folks have secrets in their lives and there's no telling what we'll find he was into. Remember my ex was laundering mob money and even I didn't know about it until he was arrested. Also, who knows what was being grown on that big farm they owned. You never know, is my point."

Tucker knew she was right and nodded toward her as he continued his search for information on the case. The Morehead City newspaper basically had the same information as yesterday with the exception of giving the victim's name. With nothing to be learned from the paper, Tucker suggested that after breakfast they drive back to the island and go by the beach house that the couple had owned. Susan had already started their meal and within a short time they were on the road back toward the island, each of them thinking about the widow and what she must be going through.

When they arrived at the house there were two Sheriff's cars on site and Tucker recognized the Sheriff as he sat in the one nearest the road talking on his car radio.

He and Susan got out of his pickup and slowly approached the Sheriff, waiting for him to finish his conversation, staying far enough away to assure his privacy. Sheriff Watson waved them closer and continued to speak to the radio. "Has the FBI returned your call? You did let them know the body was found on Federal land but we're pretty sure the actual murder took place over here at Harkers, right? I want to hear the minute they call. Watson out."

"That deputy, who happens to be my son-in-law, is just too damn lazy, but I can't fire him, you know. My daughter would just have a conniption if I did and she'd probably end up back at home, God forbid."

"Understood," said Tucker as he came close to the car. "Can you let us in to look around, Sheriff? Anything indicating that the murder was here at the house?"

Sheriff Watson answered, "Yeah, you can go inside but first let's set some guidelines about our investigation. You know more about forensic stuff than me, so you know how to handle that part. Anything we discover must remain in strictest confidence and if I find out you talked about the case I'll bust you for obstruction. I suspect this will be a shared jurisdiction case so the FBI will have to know about your involvement and it's up to you to work out details with them. Understood?"

"Understood, Sheriff. Can you tell me the Agent in Charge of this case as soon as you find out? Something else, you're in charge at all times, right?"

"We're gonna get along just fine, I think."

Tucker and Susan entered the house after the Sheriff introduced them to the deputy standing at the doorway looking rather bored. When they passed, Tucker heard the deputy grumble in a low voice, "Guess the sheriff thinks we need some help with this one." to no one in particular. Ignoring this, Tucker began to search through every room slowly looking for anything which might indicate the murder might have occurred here. Susan walked with him, trying to be a good assistant, in the vein of Stephanie Powers on Hart to Hart. As they reached the downstairs bathroom, they were met by a rather attractive young woman dressed in a gray uniform with the letters SBI on the pocket. Tucker waited patiently as she removed water from the sink drain and placed it in a small vial and wrote on the label. He knew this was an evidence bottle, and the label was to identify the location and would be used to track the contents through the lab and maintain chain of custody if anything pertinent was found.

Tucker smiled as she turned toward him and said, "Hi, I'm Tucker and this is Susan. We're just here to see if we can help a little."

The SBI Technician returned his smile and reaching out to take his hand said, "The sheriff told us about you guys, and I guess anything you can add will be good. I've found some blood residue in the sink drain down here but won't be able to tell if it's the victim's or not until we do DNA testing. In any case, it could be his blood from a shaving cut. There's not much to indicate anyone was beaten or killed here that I've found. I'm still looking though."

"Would it be OK if we looked upstairs if you're finished there."

"Sure, just wear gloves and be careful not to disturb anything. I've already looked and as I said, I've found nothing so far."

Tucker and Susan climbed the stairs in silence and spoke only after they were out of earshot of the SBI tech.

Susan said, "It looks like the SBI isn't taking this all that seriously sending only one tech and a young one at that."

"Maybe she is their best tech. Let's don't rush to judgment until we see what she finds." responded Tucker.

Susan nodded in agreement and began her own search around the room using her most serious technique based on her many hours of "Hart to Hart" reruns. After a time, she approached Tucker and said quietly, "I think the tech has probably seen everything important, what do you think?"

Tucker smiled and nodded slowly as he guided her out of the room and back down to the first floor where the others were working. They exited the house and went to talk to the Sheriff once again. Tucker briefly complimented the Sheriff on the professionalism of his crew as well as having the SBI in on the case so soon. He then reached for his tablet computer and took some notes as he casually said to the Sheriff, "Sheriff Watson, I'd like to go to New Bern with my wife and meet with the victim's wife; partly just to try and help her out but also to ask some questions, if that would be OK with you."

Sheriff Watson hesitated and chewing on his lower lip slowly answered, "I'm probably OK with that but don't you think she's had enough on her mind already. First my deputy and I expect the FBI agents in a few hours. What do you think you can learn by talking to her? Oh, by the way, the agent in charge on this for the FBI is a guy named Andy Jessup. You know him?"

Tucker couldn't suppress the smile as he answered, "Oh, yeah, we've worked together before and, if it's OK with you, I'll just call him and maybe I can be the FBI guy for him. Thanks and I'm gonna call him right now!"

# Chapter 4 Jessup Agent in Charge

When the phone rang and the caller ID indicated a call from North Carolina, Special Agent in Charge Andy Jessup, fully expected to hear a southern drawl figuring the call was about the case he just received regarding the body found on Shackleford Banks. But he didn't expect to recognize the voice and certainly didn't expect to hear Tucker, the retired cop that he'd worked with on the National Park case. He wasn't sure whether he was glad it was Tucker or just surprised.

"Tucker, what the hell do you want. No, wait, let me be polite. How've you been? Now, what the hell do you want?"

Tucker just laughed and said, "I've been OK. How about you? Any cases you can't solve without my help?" which made Jessup snort and bark back.

"Got a jaywalker that's been terrorizing DC. That's about your speed."

Tucker laughed again and began in earnest. "I know you're the AIC of the Shackleford case. You know, the murder victim from Harkers Island. I used to spend a lot of time on the island and thought maybe I might be able to help."

"We'll talk about that later. What have you been doing? You still with the pretty blond? Are you married yet?" Jessup rambled, "I hate to say it but I kinda miss your help. Too bad you're not an agent or at least a cop."

"Well, I'm working as a private investigator now. Is that close enough?" quipped Tucker. "I'd really like to work on this case for you. I'm betting you're a bit understaffed and could use some free help."

Jessup said, "Hey, free help is always good. You mean, I don't have to pay you? What are you, a millionaire?"

"Well, Susan, the blond, is and we're together now, so money is no issue. I think I'm gonna marry that gal soon. Feels like I'm finally in love again."

Jessup suddenly became serious, "I'm headed down that way tomorrow. The local office has nothing and I'm not sure they're all that good. Why don't you and Susan pick me up at the New Hanover Airport in Wilmington tomorrow? I land at 9:35 in the morning. Flight 4323. That OK? Then we can talk about all this."

"Sounds good. Why don't we plan on visiting the victim's wife in New Bern in the afternoon."

"If I let you in on this, then OK. We'll talk tomorrow morning. See you then." Jessup hung up and, rocking back in his chair, his mind returned to the last time he had seen Tucker. Shot up, beat up, and looking pretty bad. Jessup hoped that the blond was taking care of the man that, for whatever reason, he had befriended. The last case they had been on together had been just too horrendous and Jessup couldn't stand another like that. On reflection though, if Tucker had not been involved before, the body count would most likely have been much higher. He gathered his stuff for the trip to North Carolina and said a little prayer that this case would turn out much better than the last. Ever the pessimist, he doubted it!

# Chapter 5 Tucker and Jessup Together Again

Tucker and Susan arrived at the airport in Wilmington just in time to greet Jessup coming out of the gate area into the terminal. When Tucker saw him, memories of their last encounter flooded back and he shivered for a second. He had been in bad shape when they last saw each other and the memory was scary. The best thing about that had been his encounter with Susan and the developing relationship which started then. He walked rapidly and extended his hand in welcome to Jessup who responded with a vigorous shake and a big grin. Susan hung back briefly but soon came up and gave Jessup a hug.

They exchanged pleasantries as they walked toward Tucker's truck but as soon as the door closed Jessup exclaimed, "So, you're now a PI, huh!" and waited for Tucker to tell the tale. After Tucker explained what he and Susan had decided to do with their time Jessup laughed out loud and made light of the "Hart to Hart" reference.

"Well, I gotta tell ya, Tucker. Susan is at least as pretty as her role model but you got a ways to go to be Robert Wagner!"

"Yeah, but I'm a better cop." said Tucker. He then went on to explain how they got involved in this particular case and brief Jessup on everything they'd learned. He waited, giving Jessup time to digest the story, before expressing his real concern.

"Are you gonna let us in on this case. I have a lot of friends on the island and it would mean a lot to me to help find who killed this man."

"Did you know the victim? Is there any conflict there?" demanded Jessup.

"No, they're newcomers to the island."

"Well, based on your performance during the National Park thing, we can use your help. As I told you earlier, I'm not all that impressed with the locals here." Jessup stated.

Tucker barely contained his delight and after thinking for a few minutes he asked Jessup, "Are we visiting the victim's wife this afternoon? She may be able to give us some insight into enemies or possible motive."

Jessup smiled and said, "I had the local agent contact her yesterday afternoon and set up an appointment for all of us to meet her in New Bern. After I get a car from the carpool here in Wilmington, we'll drive up that way and meet at her house. You didn't think I'd pass on free help did you?"

After they'd dropped off Jessup at his local office, Tucker and Susan headed up Highway 17 toward New Bern for the meeting, stopping several times for Susan to see some local color. She was distracted and her thoughts were on the poor widow and her grief. Tucker, ever the cop, was thinking about who might have had a reason to kill this man. As a banker, wealthy enough to own a second home at the beach, and having a large farm by local standards, he was probably worth a lot and, of course, this led Tucker to consider family members. First, they needed to see who would benefit from the man's death the most. Then they needed to consider any outside persons who might want the man dead. As Susan had stated earlier, the farm might be a place where something other than tobacco or cotton was grown. Also, there was always something at the bank to consider, embezzlement, fraud, whatever. Tucker tried to close his mind to all this, knowing that Jessup was probably going down the same path and would have all the pertinent records they needed to examine waiting for them. He drove on, mostly in silence, thinking only of the upcoming interview. Susan had tears in her eyes as they entered the Stallings driveway, noticing the black sedan with federal plates indicating that Jessup was already there. They walked slowly up to the door which was immediately opened by a man in a black suit. They were whisked into a rather large living room where they saw Jessup, a man wearing a Deputy's uniform, and a small brunette woman who was sobbing into a tissue and being hugged by another suited man.

Jessup stood up and did the barest of introductions, adding that the man in the suit was Mrs. Stallings' lawyer. Tucker found this rather curious, but he withheld any comments.

Jessup then said, "We can continue now if that's all right, Mrs. Stallings? You'd said that your husband went to the island to check on your home there. Exactly when did he go down there? Was he alone?"

Mrs. Stallings wiped her tears and raising her head she said, "He went on Saturday morning after the hurricane came through. He was by himself. He only went to check on the house." She started crying again. "I told him when we bought that place it was wrong. We only live an hour away but he said it was an investment that we could enjoy while it....." she broke up and started to sob again.

The lawyer rose from the couch and spat, "Can't this wait? Can't you see she's just torn up? Maybe I can answer your questions?"

Jessup said, "Why don't you go upstairs and rest, Mrs. Stallings. We can continue this later. We'll try and get what we need from Mr. Hall."

The widow walked slowly to the staircase and up to her room where her sister was waiting to comfort her. Hall, the lawyer, turned to Jessup and said, "I know you want to talk to her but I assure you she has nothing to do with this and I believe I can provide you anything you need to know.

Tucker interrupted, "Why did she call her lawyer to be here for an interview? Does she have something to hide?"

Hall responded immediately. "Too much television. All my clients are afraid to talk to the authorities without representation, plus I've been their lawyer for over 35 years as well as a family friend. I'd be here even if Stella didn't call me."

"Understood. What can you tell us about the family?" said Jessup.

The room was quiet as Hall gathered his thoughts, trying to balance being open to the authorities with his obligation to the family. He finally decided that the best move was to be as open as possible, answering as many questions from the authorities as he could. Hall began to speak freely about the Stallings family.

As Tucker listened, he rapidly concluded that whatever had happened in the house on Harkers Island, it was not a result of any criminal enterprise that the family was involved in. These folks, based on what he had already found and confirmed by their lawyer, were the typical couple living the American dream, albeit a little better than most. When he and Jessup had concluded the interview, they met outside near their cars to briefly discuss what they had just heard.

Jessup said, "Well, I'll keep my guys looking into the family but I think we're dealing with something else. Maybe the man was robbed, you know, came on someone in the house while they were ransacking it and was killed for his effort. Maybe some drugged up squatter killed him when he tried to evict them. I need to see the crime scene next."

"Agreed, we've been to the house so Susan and I will stay around for a while and try to talk to Mrs. Stallings after she calms down. We'll contact you tomorrow." said Tucker as he grabbed Susan's hand, and they headed back toward the house. The door was opened by the Deputy who nodded solemnly and moved aside so they could enter. Mrs. Stallings had returned downstairs and was sitting quietly on the couch staring out the window at the water. Susan sat beside her and putting her arms around the distraught woman, quietly said, "We're so sorry for your loss and my husband and I will do anything we can to find out who did this. Can I ask you a few questions, if it's not too painful?"

Mrs. Stallings nodded and said, "Call me Stella, please. I'll try to help if I can." She raised her head, looking Susan in the eyes and continued, "You're not in the FBI, are you? What's your role in all this? Are you with the Morehead City police?"

Susan answered, "No, Ma'am. Tucker and I are private investigators, and Tucker has a history with folks on the island so we just want to help you any way we can, not just with the investigation."

The elderly woman raised her head and showing a brief smile said, "I really don't think hiring a private investigator is necessary and besides I'm sure our money will be tied up for some time so I couldn't pay you now."

Susan interrupted quickly and said, "No, Stella, we just want to help, no payment is necessary. This is just what we do."

"Well, I guess it won't hurt anything. I just want the man who did this caught and punished."

Susan then began to question the woman softly and with technique that amazed Tucker. She asked good questions, avoided leading comments and, in general, allowed the widow to tell her story with little guidance getting the best information possible under the circumstances.

Susan continued to ask good questions, covering a myriad of topics, all related to the family background and money without being too prying. She had taken the role of interrogator seriously and was able to make the older woman feel comfortable allowing the discovery of facts as well as attitudes. They learned of a son who'd recently returned from Afghanistan after two years as a Marine sniper and was experiencing some difficulty adjusting. They also heard about a daughter who had very expensive tastes and whose husband had recently lost his job as the manager of a local car dealership.

Susan stood, grabbed Tucker's hand, and moving toward the door, said, "Thank you for talking to us. We'll keep you informed if we find anything and again, we're so sorry for your loss."

"Thanks for your kindness. After so many of our friends on the island didn't come down this past summer, I've been really lonely, and I do appreciate your friendship and help on all this."

At length, Mrs. Stallings finished by saying, "Well, I think I need to talk to Ward right now. We have some arrangements to make for the funeral. He's been a godsend during this. I'm so glad we have him as a friend and lawyer."

Before Susan was done they knew enough about the family and circumstances to believe that whatever had happened to this man, Mrs. Stallings was not involved and was in the dark about anything he might have been involved in that could have resulted in his murder. As they drove back to the campground, they each considered what the woman was going through and felt both sad and motivated to find the killer and bring her some peace.

That evening as they sat outside the motorhome enjoying the soft ocean breeze, Tucker was moved to comment on the day's events, saying, "You know baby, you're the best. You were wonderful today questioning Stella. Just watching you was a pleasure. I need you to know that I'm pretty sure I'm falling in love with you. Is that as scary to you as it is to me?"

Susan turned to face him and said, "You know about my history with men, bad choices and all, but this time I'm convinced you're the best thing that ever happened to me. Yes, loving again is scary for me as well, but worth the nerves."

She rose from her lounge chair and, taking his hand, led him to the camper to pursue this conversation to its logical conclusion. Both of them stepped lightly up the RV stairs and inside.

# Chapter 6 Tucker Investigations, Inc.

Tucker woke with the sun the next day and quietly exited the RV after starting coffee. He wanted to walk on the beach and ponder what was happening in his life. The previous evening's events had brought into focus some things he'd been considering a lot lately. Additionally, the session with the widow the previous day had made him realize some things.

He really did miss being involved in investigations. Susan was a natural, and what he had considered might be a lark, he now realized was a calling. He and Susan needed to confirm their relationship and then get busy helping folks like Stella Stallings. They'd both wasted enough time in their lives and starting right now needed to begin paying back the world for their good fortune. He resolved, as he walked along the empty beach, to ask Susan to marry him that very day and if she agreed, he wanted them to form a partnership they would call Tucker Investigations. He turned and began walking faster and faster as he returned to the RV. His smile grew wider as he walked.

Susan was up and sitting outside at the picnic table with her coffee when he returned. She could tell something was up with the big ole grin he was showing as she rose to get him some coffee. Tucker could barely contain himself as he took the cup and sat down, turning toward Susan with a mischievous look.

"How are you this morning, love? Are you awake yet?"

Susan responded, "Yes, what's going on? Where've you been? Are you OK?"

"I'm actually very ok," said Tucker, "I was thinking that when I apply for the PI license maybe we should apply as a team. You were very good yesterday with the questioning and I'd like you to be an investigator as well; sound OK?"

Susan, in the spirit of the moment, grinned and said, "You didn't think I'd let you go on this adventure with me only in the background, did you? Of course I want to be a Private Investigator as well. I'm Jennifer Hart, you know."

Tucker continued, "The paperwork for being a PI is pretty involved and requires a visit to the courthouse." He then dropped from his seat and knelt, continuing, "Maybe while we're there we should get another license as well, you know, since we'll be there already."

The look on Susan's face was classic; stunned, confused, and happy at the same time. Taking only a few seconds, she answered, "If you're talking about a gun license for me, I'll shoot you. If you're talking about a marriage license, I love you!"

They embraced as only good friends and lovers can and giggling like teenagers went inside the RV, closing the door with a bang and moving to the bedroom to celebrate the new life they were entering.

Later that day the pair went into Morehead City to begin their journey together as a PI couple. After standing in line at the courthouse for what seemed like hours, they filled out the necessary paperwork to obtain PI licenses and then moving to another window got their marriage license. After a brief discussion, they decided to wait for a better time to actually get the ceremony performed and headed toward Harkers Island to try to piece together what had happened there. They traveled in silence, both considering the implications of their actions that morning, each a bit nervous at what was transpiring but convinced they were doing the right thing and would spend the rest of their lives together.

As they crossed the bridge to the island, Tucker spoke, “I think we should talk to Ralph. He called earlier to say he knew Stallings, and I let him know we were working on the case. The FBI has interviewed the neighbors, and we can get what we can from their interviews later. I’d like to have Ralph’s take on all this, you agree?”

Susan started from her daydream to agree with him as they approached Bob’s and turned into the parking lot. Tucker opened his door hurriedly and ran around the truck to open the passenger door for Susan saying, “Allow me my love; might as well start spoiling my lovely bride right now.”

“I love your southern gentlemen ways but I’m quite capable of opening my own door, thank you. Sweet, but unnecessary.” They walked hand in hand into the store to talk to Ralph.

# Chapter 7 The Case Evolves

As he entered the store, Tucker saw Ralph working in the checkout lane bagging for an elderly couple who were apparently stocking up their larder. Ralph was joking with the couple saying, "If you guys came a little more often, like you used to, you wouldn't have to start off with everything new each visit. Say, when were you down last, it's been close to a year, right?"

The woman looked up at Ralph with a somber expression and said, "We couldn't come all last year. We were robbed at our home and after that we just couldn't bear to leave the house empty. We were afraid we'd get robbed so we stayed around hoping the police would catch who did it. They never did and so we decided to install a security system and hope for the best."

Ralph sighed and said, "Bad deal. You're OK though and that's a blessing. What happened?"

Tucker edged closer and listened intently, the cop in him on the alert. Susan stood at his side and listened as well.

The husband interrupted the conversation saying, "Someone just broke down our back door and got in. They ransacked the house but only took cash and jewelry. Then they wrote a note on my computer telling us to be watchful in the future. The exact words, which I'll never forget, were, "This could happen again at any time so be vigilant. Empty houses are our treasures." Really odd and it kept us home for a while. Like Louise said, we finally ended up putting in a security system and coming on down here anyways."

Tucker turned to Susan with a bewildered look and then touched Ralph on his shoulder. Ralph turned and with a grin, introduced the couples.

Tucker realized then that he'd met the couple when he'd been here before, Louise and Joseph Walker. He and Susan walked them to their car as Ralph returned to his work at the cash register. Tucker and Susan returned to the store after the Walkers left and found Ralph waiting at the door, having assigned his duties to the young lady assisting him. They went to the small, raised office area to discuss the Stallings murder.

Ralph began the conversation with an apology for making them wait but was soon interrupted by Susan who said, "Oh no, that was a fascinating story. Who ever heard of a burglar leaving a victim a warning? Wouldn't have missed that tale for anything."

Tucker agreed and they moved on to the case at hand.

Ralph started, "Like I told you on the phone, I knew the Stallings. Nice folks and as far as I know not an enemy in the world. At least not down here. Can't say about back in New Bern. I heard that George got down here the day after the hurricane and went straight to his house. I'm pretty sure he was alone when he got here. He never came by the store and far as I've heard just went to his house and went inside. Wish I could help more, but that's really all I know. Kinda hard to believe anyone would kill such a nice guy, especially here on the island."

Tucker asked. "Any reason to think he made someone mad here on the island? Property disputes, neighbor arguments, that sorta thing?"

"Nope, he wasn't the type to argue, he was more the get-along-at-any-cost type, odd for such a rich man, really. Maybe some folks were jealous that he owned a couple of houses here on the island and was getting ready to buy another one from one of the locals. Hardly any reason to kill him though."

Tucker considered this momentarily and then turning to Susan said, "You got anything, honey? What else do we need to know?"

Susan said, "Ralph, have you heard any more stories like the one that Louise and her husband went through? I'm just curious!"

"I did talk to another couple from Greensboro who'd been burglarized. Didn't mention a note though. I'll ask when they come in."

"Could we have their names so we could ask now?" asked Susan, and Ralph wrote the name and address on a yellow pad and handed it over.

As Tucker and Susan walked toward their truck, Tucker turned to Susan and said, "What was that all about?"

Susan smiled and quietly replied, "Just an idea I had. I'll tell you if it pans out. Probably nothing, but you never know."

After driving around the island for a time, they headed back to the mainland, considering what they'd learned. Everyone who knew Stallings thought he was a good man. No one knew anything to explain the murder of such a person. No one knew anything about him that might be a motive for his murder. As the sun was getting low in the west causing the sky to turn blood red, they arrived in Morehead City. It was the proper time for an early dinner so they stopped at a chain restaurant to eat.

It'd been a long and eventful day, and after a relaxing meal of seafood and cold beer, the couple returned to their camper for the evening.

# Chapter 8 Complications

Earlier than normal Tucker's cell rang and the caller ID indicated it was Jessup. When he answered, he selected speaker phone so Susan could listen in. He heard an exasperated sounding Jessup exclaim, "The State Bureau forensics tech found nothing in the house to help us. Either the murder was done elsewhere, or the perp was a real artist with the cleanup. Basically, we're nowhere. Nothing useful on the body, nothing at the house, and we'll never learn anything on Shackleford Banks since the hurricane completely scoured the area. I'm going back to Washington tonight and leaving this one to the locals. If they turn anything up, I've told them to let you in on it. Sheriff Watson also agreed to tell you everything he learns. Good luck with this one, if you keep at it. It's a bad one."

Tucker looked at Susan before responding and then said, "Susan has an idea we want to pursue. So, I think we're gonna stay the course. We might be Mrs. Stallings' best hope of closure on this thing. I'll keep in touch." Jessup grunted, then rang off, as he usually did without saying goodbye.

Later that morning Tucker's cell rang again. When he saw it was a local number, Tucker jumped quickly to answer expecting to hear Ralph's voice and was surprised when he heard, "This is Sheriff Watson. That you, Tucker?"

"Yeah, what's up Sheriff? News?"

Watson spoke softly but clearly. "Can you come see me this morning? I've got something you might want to see and we need to talk. Get here as soon as you can, OK?"

———————————————————

As they drove toward town, both Susan and Tucker were racking their brains trying to figure what Watson might have found but after a while simply decided to give up and wait until they arrived. The deputy escorted them directly to the Sheriff's office and they sat down after getting the coffee they'd missed in their hurry to get there. Sheriff Watson came into the room and, sitting behind his desk said, "We found something in Stallings' garage that could turn out to be important. Thought you might want to know before you get too involved in all this, trying to help the widow and all. In a small fireproof safe, attached under the floor, there was over $30 thousand dollars in cash; small bills, used, the kind of money you'd find on a drug dealer. Not what you'd expect to find at a banker's house, you know. Might be that when we find why the money is there, we might figure out why Stallings was killed and then who did it."

Tucker and Susan looked at each other and then at the Sheriff with shocked expressions. This entire situation had changed with the discovery of the money. While this might be innocent, the odds were that there was a connection between the cash and the murder. Each thought to themselves, ' so much for a nice family man with nothing to hide.'

The Sheriff continued, "We're gonna focus on Stallings' local contacts. I told Agent Jessup and he's gonna check on the personal and business finances. At least we've got something to work on now, even if we don't like where this is headed. Thought you'd want to know."

Tucker asked, "Have you told the widow about this yet? We might want to confront her face to face to judge her reaction."

"No, haven't told her yet. I thought maybe your wife might be the best to do that. This afternoon if you can."

Tucker and Susan were both apprehensive as they traveled toward New Bern, for their apparent misreading of the Stallings situation, and they were also wondering how the widow would take this news. If she was aware of the cash and it was something above board then this would be an easy and short meeting, otherwise, it could get testy and certainly uncomfortable for all involved. When they arrived, Tucker said, "Honey, you take the lead on this, and I'll try to just observe."

Mrs. Stallings was quick to greet them at her door and started the conversation by asking if they had found anything thus far. At that, Susan asked her to sit down, and they all went into the living room and sat facing each other. Susan began. "Mrs. Stallings, Stella, the police discovered something interesting at your place on the island. Are you aware of any reason your husband might have large sums of cash stored there? They found around thirty thousand dollars in a safe hidden in the storage building out back."

Mrs. Stallings face became blank, and it was easy to see she was struggling with this news. It appeared to take her by surprise, indicating either she knew nothing, or was shocked that it had been found.

Mrs. Stallings at last said, "My husband never used cash unless it was absolutely necessary. I can't imagine what this much would be for. Where could he have gotten it? Oh my God, what was he doing?"

Susan grasped her hand and said calmly, "I'm sure there's a good explanation; we just needed to know if you could help us figure it out. We'll leave you now, but we'll keep in touch. Oh, there's one more thing. Who had access to your beach house besides you and your husband?"

"Well, our kids of course, and the neighbor behind had a spare key to check on it for us. Mr. Gamble. He's lived there all his life and helps all the neighbors that way. Why?"

"Just trying to figure out if maybe the cash wasn't your husband's, and someone stashed it there."

Susan and Tucker left with that and began the long trek back to the coast. As they drove, Tucker called the Sheriff to make sure they were checking the safe and the money for prints and was assured it was in process. Tucker told him about the meeting with Mrs. Stallings and the belief that he and Susan shared that Stella was unaware of the cash. Sheriff Watson agreed to call as soon as he had word about the prints.

When they arrived back at the Emerald Isle campsite, they both agreed that it was too late in the day to continue any useful work on the case and decided to visit the beach and do a little fishing and sunbathing. Susan dressed in her bathing suit and Tucker donned his typical fishing apparel, trunks and an old tee shirt. The wide white beach was bare when they arrived and wasting no time, within minutes Tucker was casting into the surf in anticipation of the big one. He hoped to catch a blue in the surf this time of year and he began to cast and retrieve the silver spoon he'd used for years. Within minutes he had a good one on and he heard Susan call out, "Need any help, big boy?"

Tucker merely grunted and continued to reel in the big bluefish. Within minutes he had the fish on shore and was bleeding it to preserve the freshness for their evening meal. The afternoon passed rather quickly, and the couple found themselves back in their campsite having had a great meal, discussing the case as the sun set casting long shadows onto the beach.

"So do you think the cash they found had anything to do with the murder?"

Tucker's answer was typical cop. "No such thing as coincidence in this world. You bet it had something to do with it. Maybe the killer knew about the money and killed Stallings after beating him trying to find where it was hidden. Maybe it's drug money. Maybe he embezzled from a bank customer and they found out and killed him. Lots of possibilities, but for sure the money is involved."

Susan replied. "You really don't think that Stella knew about the money though. She seemed so surprised. As surprised as we were."

"No, I don't think she knew. Whatever it was, it was something only Stallings and perhaps the person that murdered him knew. We might know more when we get prints off the money and the safe."

At that the conversation waned and they both knew it was time to retire and continue this the next morning, with clear minds.

# Chapter 9 Forensic Failure

The day began with a beautiful orange glow in the east over the ocean accompanied by a light salty breeze that barely stirred the trees around the campsite. Susan was up first and by the time Tucker had risen she had prepared a great southern breakfast she knew he would love. She used an old southern grits casserole recipe but did the California healthy thing to it. If they were to get married, she wanted him to be around a long time; it was really love, after all. This was accompanied by the mandatory biscuits to round out the meal. She figured too much health at one time might scare him. They ate in silence, sitting at the picnic table outside their RV contemplating what the day would bring. As they enjoyed their second cup of coffee, Susan casually reminded Tucker of his need to check in with Agent Jessup about this latest development regarding the cash at the Stallings home. Tucker glanced at his watch, checking the time, and reached for his cell to call Jessup.

The phone only rang twice before Jessup answered with, "You give up already? Told you it would be a tough one."

Tucker chuckled and said, "Nope, we're still on it. Did the Sheriff let you know about the money they found at Stallings' house?" Without waiting for any response, Tucker continued. "He said you guys were checking into Stallings' financials and I was wondering what you might have found out."

"Yeah, I know about the money, my guys down there let me know. We found nothing out of the ordinary about the financial situation with Stallings. If it was his and it was legal he must have been squirreling it away for years. No sudden stock sales, no withdrawals from any accounts, nothing funny about the way his farm was going. The only thing I can think of is he had some source of cash we're unaware of. It smells like drug money to me. Maybe that house on the canal was used for more than a weekend retreat."

Tucker thought about all this for a few moments and then said, "That doesn't really fit for me. Based on her reaction, the widow was clueless about that money. Have any fingerprints been ID'd? Maybe that'll tell us something."

Jessup responded, "The only prints the SBI found on the safe were Stallings. The money, of course, had tons of smeared prints and even some traces of cocaine present on several bills. That's really meaningless as far as money goes. Bottom line, we learned nothing of note."

Tucker thanked Jessup for the input and said he'd be in touch if he and Susan got anywhere with the case. They hung up.

Tucker was baffled with the direction this case was going and briefly considered that maybe he and Susan had bitten off more than they could chew. He immediately changed his mind when Susan reminded him about how they'd met in the middle of a confusing series of murders which he had pursued relentlessly to the end. He realized that the more difficult a case seemed at the outset the more the people involved needed his help and the more it made him want to help. They finished their coffee and spent some time just enjoying the ocean and the beautiful day at the beach, realizing that the state and local authorities needed more time to process evidence and gather information before any of them could continue effectively.

Tucker used his computer to research the local area in hopes of finding some details about the island that might help them with the case.

Susan busied herself with organizing their camper for the stay here at the beach. Since they arrived, their focus had been on becoming investigators and she realized that there needed to be some life going on, not just police work. She was so glad that their relationship had evolved to a point where silence and individual focus were acceptable. She was quietly working and suddenly realized that she was as happy as she'd ever been, both with Tucker and with her life in general.

After a time, Susan turned her mind to the events of the last few days and decided to pursue her hunch about the burglaries they'd heard about while visiting Ralph at the grocery store. Opening her laptop she connected to the internet, knowing this would take quite a while, but determined to follow through on her idea.

The day passed quickly as they were each busy with gathering information and soon it was evening in the campground. As the shadows lengthened and the day was ending, they almost simultaneously said it was time for dinner. With each too busy to cook, a nice meal in town seemed to be appropriate. Driving toward Morehead City Tucker commented, "I've found out some things about the local area that might help us on the Stallings case. What kept you so busy all afternoon? You were really intent with whatever you were into."

Susan thought for a few seconds before answering. At last she said, "I'm think I'm onto something odd but most likely not associated with the Stallings case. Remember the burglaries we heard about? There is something really strange going on here, I believe."

Just then they arrived at the restaurant they'd decided on and the conversation was interrupted while Tucker parked the truck.

They went into the lobby where a young lady, speaking with the dialect so indicative of the area said, "Dinner for two? This way please," then led them to a booth with a wonderful view of the docks. The fishing boats tied up in several rows, surrounded by all the tall lights made it a peaceful scene. Tucker, after ordering a glass of white wine for each of them, asked Susan, "What did you find so odd?"

"Well, you told me about coincidences in police work, remember? I spent the afternoon looking at databases of folks that come to the island but don't live here. Dingbatters, you called them. It was pretty easy to find those guys looking at utility records, real estate records; that sort of thing."

Tucker interrupted. "You never cease to amaze me. How'd you know how to do that? Never mind, I'll just appreciate that you can."

Susan smiled saying, "You don't think I'm just a pretty face, do you? In a past life I spent a lot of time online and took a few classes on programming. You remember my last ex-husband was an accountant. I helped him at the beginning of his career. Anyways, I looked into the hometowns of several of the many Dingbatters and found out that a big chunk of them have been burglarized in the last two years in their real homes. They are, of course, mostly wealthy and you might think likely to be robbed but I mean a lot more than would be normal. I'm talking maybe 20% or more of the ones I looked at. Odd, at least, don't you think?"

Tucker nodded in agreement and asked, "What about the message the first couple got? Any more of them in this group?"

"In two cases the local authorities put in their reports that a note had been found but they didn't comment on what it said."

Tucker's response confirmed what Susan had thought. "Cops do that sometimes just to have something held back to verify if they caught the right guy and to tell if they get a false confession from some whacko. Only the thieves would know what was in the notes."

The couple sat in silence for a while and eventually their food arrived. Eating occupied the next several minutes but finally Susan asked, "What did you find out? Was Stallings a drug dealer or something?"

"I didn't find anything on Stallings, specifically, but about something going on with the island that he might have been a part of. You remember seeing the gated community we passed as we drove around that looked like it had fizzled out?" Susan nodded and waited for him to continue. "Well, I figured the economy being what it is lately, that the money just ran out and the developers put everything on hold looking for financing. It seems that's not the case at all. The developer, who's out of New Bern, has good financing but a local resident came up with an old document, dating back to the Civil War, that identifies the property as a cemetery used by the Union sailors and soldiers that held the island for most of the war. This makes the area a historic landmark and stopped the development in its tracks. Until this issue is resolved, the developer is on hold and can't continue building and certainly can't sell the land. It must be costing them a fortune."

Tucker paused to finish his wine, then continued, "If Stallings was involved in any of this, we may have found a motive. Most bribes are made in cash."

"Have you told Jessup about this? The FBI could tell pretty fast if Stallings was involved legally."

"Yes, I emailed Andy this afternoon. He might've responded by the time we get back to the campsite. He'll probably have us follow up with the widow again if he finds anything implicating Stallings. He's really down on his people here. We'll see!"

They ate the remainder of the meal without speaking and soon were heading toward the RV, anxious to see what the FBI had found. Just as they got back, Tucker's cell rang and recognizing Jessup's ring, he answered quickly. After several minutes he ended the call with a "Yeah, we're on it." and turned to face Susan, who'd been listening intently the entire time.

"As far as the FBI can determine Stallings was only indirectly involved in this particular land deal as a minor investor in the Dunes Resort Group, but they did discover that he'd been negotiating on another property quite close to the development that could have been affected if the area remained a historical landmark. Like I said earlier, bribes are paid in cash whether to a government guy or anyone else. We'll need to talk to the widow ASAP. Jessup gave us his blessing and the Sheriff will agree, I'm sure."

# Chapter 10 Money or Real Estate

After calling Mrs. Stallings and arranging a meeting the next morning to discuss the pending land purchase, they headed back to New Bern. On their arrival, they found that Mrs. Stallings had called her friend and lawyer Hall to attend this meeting with her. Assuming the worst, Tucker told Susan he would lead this interrogation, for interrogation it was now, rather than friendly acquisition of information, when a lawyer was involved. He wondered why the situation had changed so rapidly but soon discovered the reason with his first inquiry.

"Mrs. Stallings, we're here to see what you knew about a real estate deal your husband was working on when he was killed. Were you aware of his interest in purchasing land near the development off Oak Grove Street on the island?"

"I was involved in the negotiations since I'd become friends with the couple that owned the land. Mr. Hall has advised me against saying any more than that at this time, so I'm afraid you may have traveled here for no reason."

Tucker merely nodded and turning to Hall said, "I'm sure you have some reason to keep her silent but you know we can subpoena her if we have to. Why not just make this easy on all of us and let her talk?"

"Mr. Tucker, you **are not** with the authorities and have no power to subpoena anyone. You may not know it, but real estate deals that are incomplete can be ruined by innocent remarks. For the sake of Mrs. Stallings' future financial security, we need to keep the details of this transaction quiet until documentation has been signed assuring secrecy or the transaction is complete, which I believe will take some time. I'll let you know when the appropriate parties have been notified and secrecy assured. I apologize for you making a wasted trip but the short notice did not allow me sufficient time to make it work."

With that, Hall rose and made it apparent the meeting was over. Tucker and Susan shook hands with the pair and let themselves out the front door. As they walked toward their truck Tucker muttered so only Susan could hear, "Damn lawyers, just delaying the inevitable." even though he knew that Hall had a point about real estate deals and secrecy. They headed back, each lost in their own thoughts. After some time Susan commented, "I still think that Stella isn't involved in any of this!"

Tucker responded after some thought, "You're probably right, but we should reserve judgment until all the information is in. I've been fooled by naïve, innocent acting people before. She may be the mastermind and it's up to us to find out. We're in this case for ourselves now, not for her, no matter how we got involved."

Susan retorted, "I know, but she's so nice. I just know she's telling the truth. So, what now?"

# Chapter 11 Robberies

By the time they had finished the drive back from the mainland to the beach, Susan had talked Tucker into visiting the couple that was burglarized Ralph had told them about earlier. They drove around the island slowly, noting the contrast between the Dingbatters typically large homes and the local residents older, smaller, somewhat run down residences. When they arrived at an even larger than typical house on the sound side of the island, Susan said, "Let me ask the questions this time, please. I'll tell you what I'm getting at after I hear what they have to say. It's probably nothing, like I said."

Tucker agreed to let her lead the way and they walked up the long path toward the house and rang the bell. They heard movement inside and after a few moments the door opened slightly and a petite, rather neat looking woman, who appeared to be in her sixties, peered out.

She said, "May I help you?" in a somewhat tentative voice keeping the door chained like an inner-city resident.

Susan explained who they were, how they knew her name, and what they wanted and eventually persuaded the woman to open the door and talk to them. When they'd settled on the couch and been served coffee, Susan opened the conversation.

"Mrs. Garrison, as I said, we heard you were robbed at your home in Greensboro several months ago. Has anything happened since then? Have they solved the crime or recovered anything that was stolen?"

Mrs. Garrison answered, "Nothing yet. The thieves only took money and some gold that was impossible to identify. The police said there was very little chance of finding out who did it or ever recovering anything. We pretty much gave up soon after the break in."

"Was there anything else you could add? Anything odd that happened?" Susan asked and Tucker suddenly saw where this was leading.

"Well, a few days after the break in, we got a letter in the mail saying this could happen again and something about our house being a treasure. We told the police about it but they said it was a prank and we should forget it. Seemed like they were right, so that's what we did. Why?"

"Just a hunch," said Susan. "Did you keep the letter or the envelope? We sure would like to see it."

"I did but, it's back in Greensboro. I could send it to you when we go back home. We're leaving in just a few days. Weather's turning chilly, you know!"

Susan said, "We really want to see it and we just happen to be going to Greensboro next week. Could we maybe meet you at your home and see it then? We can have the local police meet us there if you'd be more comfortable." She caught Tucker's eye and winked.

"I suppose that would be ok. We'll be home by next Wednesday. You can get our address off the internet and please do bring the local police. Detective Lineberry was on our case. The Greensboro Police Department, of course."

Susan rose and taking Tucker's hand said, "We can escort ourselves out. Thanks and we'll see you Wednesday afternoon around three o'clock if that's OK?"

"That'll be fine. Goodbye."

They walked out to their truck in silence until they were driving away. Tucker broke the silence when he said, "I finally understand what you've been thinking. Pretty smart, I have to say.

These events have to be connected. Looks like we're going to Greensboro. There's really nothing happening here until Jessup and his crew get us all the background data we need to work with. You think that the Stallings murder is connected somehow?"

"I think we have to check these robberies out. There's nothing to follow up on with the murder case and we might be able to help these other folks out. At least give them some peace of mind. Maybe something will break about the murder while we're gone. I really do think there is some connection between all these things. You don't mind a little side trip to Greensboro, do you?"

Tucker nodded and reflected to himself on his luck in finding this woman. She might be a better investigator than he was and working with her and living with her was making his life better than it had been for years. Thinking about Susan and his good fortune these days, a little grin appeared behind his neatly trimmed salt and pepper beard.

"Sounds good to me. In the meantime, let's finish the PI license application and get legal with all this investigation stuff. Jessup will be finishing the background checks, financials, that kind of stuff on Stallings and Sheriff Watson will do the legwork here on the island to see if anyone saw or knows anything. Greensboro might pay off and they won't be going there. Even if there is no connection, as you said, we can help these folks as well."

That afternoon the couple went back to the Sheriff's office and Watson committed to OK the application for a PI license and gave them a letter of introduction on county letterhead, agreeing to vouch for them if anyone called for verification. With all this arranged, Tucker and Susan returned to their RV for a peaceful evening.

The next day they returned to Harkers Island to talk to the couple they'd met in Bob's about their robbery. There they found out from the neighbors that the couple had suddenly left for their home back on the mainland without saying anything to anyone. Tucker thought this very odd, as they'd been shopping the day before. After some convincing, he was able to talk the neighbor into telling him where the couple was from. They would visit the couple on their way to meet the Garrisons in Greensboro. Deciding to wait until the next morning, they returned to their RV and began to prepare for departure, opting to leave the RV and drive in the pickup.

# Chapter 12 Mainland Oddities

As luck would have it, the Walkers lived just a few miles off the interstate in Burlington which meant that the diversion off the trip to Greensboro was minimal. Tucker had called Sheriff Watson and had him try to contact the Walkers and arrange a meeting but the Sheriff had been unsuccessful. He'd told Tucker their home number simply rang continuously when he called, not allowing him to leave a message. Tucker decided to chance an unannounced visit and had Susan locate their home address on the internet as they drove. Tucker realized how well off the Walkers must be when they turned into a community with homes of at least 6000 square feet on full acre lots. Dotting the driveways were Mercedes, Porsches, Hummers, and other evidence indicating the affluence of the residents. Tucker issued a low whistle as he glanced around, saying jokingly, "Must be a neighborhood of accountants, huh, dear."

This was much funnier to Tucker than Susan and she made her irritation known saying, "Or crooked cops."

They turned to face each other and smiling said simultaneously, "Love You!"

Slowing the truck to a crawl, they followed the online driving directions back into the neighborhood until they came to a carcass of a home, burned and gutted, barely standing, at the address they were searching for. Tucker recognized the Walkers as they stood on the sidewalk in front of what had been their home, clutching each other and appearing dazed. Not knowing what to do, they parked and walked up to the couple remaining silent waiting for a reaction.

After some time, Tom Walker turned and extended his hand to Tucker saying, "Hell of a mess, huh. What brings you guys here?

Not firebugs, I hope!" He struggled to laugh but failed and simply turned back to the smoldering pile with a grim look on his face. His wife merely sobbed quietly on his shoulder.

After a time, Mrs. Walker composed herself and trying to smile, turned to Susan and said, "I guess we won't have to worry about burglars here anymore."

Susan continued to stare at the wreckage and eventually commented, "We were trying to talk to you about that and found out you'd left Harkers Island suddenly. That's why we're here. We're so sorry for your loss. At least you weren't here when it happened. Have they figured out what started the fire?"

"The fire marshal's pretty sure it started in the garage and he thinks it was arson. Why would anyone do this to us?" Mrs. Walker began to sob again.

Tucker observed, "The world is full of crazies. Maybe he just wanted to see something burn. Maybe jealous of your success. Maybe just nuts. We're on our way to Greensboro today and stopped by. When you feel up to it we'd like to talk to you again about the burglary. If it's OK?"

"Sure, here's my business card. Call me on my cell." said Mr. Walker.

As Tucker and Susan drove away, they talked about what a strange coincidence this fire was, neither really believing it was really a coincidence. After some time, Tucker said to no one in particular, "We need to see the police about burglary and the fire before we go back to the beach."

The remaining distance to Greensboro passed quickly and soon they arrived at the large, quite imposing Garrison home. It was located in an older neighborhood surrounding a golf course Tucker remembered from the Greater Greensboro Open Golf

Tournament from years back. Mr. and Mrs. Garrison greeted them warmly and, after introductions all around, offered coffee and cake. When everyone, including Detective Lineberry, whom the Garrisons had invited, was seated around the dinette table, Mrs. Garrison brought out the envelope and the note for inspection, removing them from a zip lock baggie. There appeared to be nothing unusual, white copy paper, printed with a printer, no signature, wording identical to the note the Walkers had received even the treasures part. Tucker asked, "How many folks do you think have touched it since you got it? Just you guys?"

"Yeah, just us," came the reply from the man. "We were careful in case the cops ever wanted it. Detective Lineberry never saw the need. Do you want to take it and get it tested?"

Tucker returned the papers to the baggie and said, "We'll have the FBI check it out for us. We could get lucky." He paused, then continued, "If that's OK with you, Detective."

"Our case is closed, feel free." he replied. "So you guys are consultants for the FBI, I'm told, and private investigators. Been doing it long?"

Tucker took the lead. "I'm a retired cop from Salisbury, just down the road. We've helped the FBI before."

Lineberry's expression betrayed his resentment. "Well, we did what was necessary on a simple burglary. If there's more to it, let me know."

He rose and headed toward the door saying, "I can show myself out. See you guys."

Tucker waited until the door closed and then facing the group he said, "I'm guessing we won't get much help there. Sorry the situation is so tense."

Mr. Garrison merely shrugged and said, "He's a nice guy but really, they didn't do much to solve the case. Not big enough, I suppose. We're glad to have you guys involved and thanks. Maybe the mystery of the note will be cleared up, and that would be great. We do still worry if anything else is likely to happen. Makes our trips to the beach not quite as peaceful, worrying about the place here."

Susan injected, "Do you guys keep in touch with any other DIngbatters from Harkers Island? Have any of them been robbed that you know of?"

The Garrisons faced each other momentarily before the woman said, "Well, we know a man from Winston Salem that doesn't visit down there a lot but owns several houses on the island. He was burglarized maybe a month or so after we were. Why?"

"Just something I'm trying to get straight. If it's pertinent, I'll let you know. Could you tell us his name and how to get in touch with him?"

Mr. Garrison went to a bookshelf nearby and produced a notebook which he opened and handed to Susan indicating the specific person listed with his finger. As Susan copied down the information she asked, "Did you folks know the Walkers from Burlington? They have a second home on Harkers Island as well."

Mrs. Garrison replied they didn't know anyone by that name, glancing at her husband for confirmation. He agreed, shaking his head.

Susan continued, "How about the Stallings from New Bern? Know them?"

Both of the Garrisons said, "Yes, we knew George." Mr. Garrison continued, "He was a good man. I couldn't believe anyone would kill him. Hope they catch the SOB!"

"We're helping the FBI on that case and we will catch the killer." Tucker said. "How well did you know Mr. Stallings? Did you know anything about his business dealings on the island? What kind of man was he?"

Mr. Garrison replied, "Nice as can be. I know he was looking into buying some more property on the island but I don't know why. Do you think he was killed over that?"

"We don't think anything yet. Just filling in some background. We have to look at everything. Did you folks spend time with the couple?

Garrison answered, "Not really, just occasionally. We went to dinner once in a great while with them, but no, not really that close. I only knew about the land deal because he asked me once if I knew the owners of that particular spot, but I didn't."

Tucker looked at Susan and they both rose to leave. Tucker turned toward Garrison and said, "Thanks for the information and we'll keep in touch if we find out anything about the note. We'll let you know about the Stallings case as well, as it progresses. Have a pleasant evening."

They walked silently down the drive and headed down the interstate toward Winston Salem to meet the other robbery victim, if they could arrange it. Susan tried to call the man and left a message asking that he call back.

# Chapter 13 The Bells

Josiah Bell had lived on Harkers Island all his life, well, not all of it yet, but that was his plan. As a boat builder and commercial fisherman, he was the stereotypical Harkers resident. His seventy-seven years on the island had spanned decades filled with many changes to the local character. It had moved from a quiet, isolated community of closely related residents with little outside contact to an active small town when the bridge was built in 1941, forever altering the life of the islanders. Now the island was bustling with activity as part time residents came and went with the seasons and wooden boat building, long the island's mainstay employment, was rapidly becoming a lost art. As one of the last holdouts, Josiah represented the best of old Harkers Island and was both enthusiastic and vocal in his objection to the invasion of "Dingbatters" from the mainland.

He was effectively the leader of the loosely organized group that periodically met and complained to each other about the lifestyle changes that were being forced on local residents. This group was comprised mainly of lifelong residents, mostly fishermen and boat builders, but also had a couple of local decoy artists as well. The group was active in local elections and that was basically the extent of their actions, hardly an effective lobby, but satisfying to most residents who felt they had to do something to hold on to their old life.

Josiah Bell's family consisted of four sons, two daughters, and six grandchildren after his wife had died back in 1984 of cancer. His five oldest children had moved off the island as they came of age, leaving the youngest son to carry on the family traditions. That son, Abner, called Ab by all who knew him, had moved into the house next to his parents' home place as was the way in most of the south and certainly in Eastern North Carolina. Ab was now in his fifties and had fathered two boys of his own; Tom, who was twenty-one and, Billy, who was eighteen. Both were boat builders and fisherman, though perhaps not as dedicated or focused as their father. All these Bells were active in the local isolationist political group that Josiah led.

Josiah heard his phone ring much too early that cool October morning. After a few rings he was able to clear his head and answer. He heard a muffled voice on the other end say, "You awake, old man? I need to talk to you this morning, if you got time. I'll spring for biscuits."

"Who the hell is calling at this ungodly hour? Is that you, Chuck?" Josiah at last recognized the voice of his best friend, another boat builder he worked with occasionally. "What do you want?"

Charles Barnes answered, "It's me. Can I come over now so we can talk? Like I said, I'll bring you a biscuit and coffee."

As Josiah lived alone, he often avoided cooking breakfast, as Chuck was well aware, and had to admit that a biscuit sounded good right now. "Bring two country ham and egg biscuits for me and I'll have coffee waiting. OK?"

"See you in a while."

Josiah climbed out of the rusty iron bed that had been in his family for over a hundred years and rose, hearing the sound of his old bones popping as he stood up. He went to the bathroom, added to the back of the house during a renovation he'd paid for with the proceeds of selling part of his land to a "Dingbatter" many years ago when the island was just beginning to be sought after by the wealthy mainlanders. Of course, he'd not known that it would turn into an invasion and that land prices would skyrocket as the invasion grew. If he sold that small parcel now he could build a new house with the money, rather than add a bathroom to the ole home place. After his bathroom visit, he went to the kitchen to make coffee for him and Chuck.

Glancing around, he was reminded that the whole house needed upgrading but with boat work very slow and fishing almost nonexistent, his choices now were to sell the old place and move to the mainland or to simply exist, eking out a living with what he had and what little that Social Security gave him. He just couldn't consider moving at this stage of his life so he'd accepted that this hard life was his lot and he'd hold on as long as he could pay the taxes and keep the old place livable. His mainland children were constantly after him to move in with them, but he simply would not do that as long as he was mobile. Old man's pride, he supposed.

Just as the coffee was finishing, he heard the front doorbell ring and yelled, "Come on in, Chuck. Doors open."

"Where's the coffee? Here's your biscuits, old man." Chuck called as he came into the kitchen. Chuck was only two years younger than Josiah but took advantage of every opportunity to remind Josiah of the age difference, calling him "old man" since they had dropped out of high school together over sixty years ago to become fishermen. Chuck had a similar story to that of Josiah but was fortunate to have his wife with him. Josiah often wondered how the two of them lived off what they made knowing how hard it was for him all alone. Lots of beans and rice, most likely. Of course, Chuck didn't drink and that was one of Josiah's larger expenses, even drinking the cheap stuff.

Josiah poured two cups of coffee, sweetening his but leaving Chuck's alone as was his preference. He said, "All right, what's so all fired important?"

Chuck rubbed his almost bald head and looking into Josiah's eyes asked, "Have you heard about that Dingbatter that got killed? I think your grandsons have sold him some shrimp over the last few years."

"Yeah, I heard. Nice guy. Hated to hear it but what's that got to do with me."

"Nothing, I reckon, but cops and some investigator folks are talking to people all over the island. I just thought you might want to know. Ain't your grandsons kinda into some, shall we say, shady doin's?"

Josiah considered his next comments. "Not really. They might poach a little and maybe keep the wrong fish sometimes, but I don't think the cops will be checking on all that."

Chuck frowned and said, "Ok. Just thought you might give them a warning that the cops might talk to them about the times they put ashore on that land the DIngbatter was fixin' to buy, you know near the old Union Cemetery."

Josiah chewed his country ham biscuit slowly and took his time before speaking. He sipped his coffee and said, "Oh that was nothing. They was just looking for something from the old days to sell on E bay. Nothing, really!"

"If you say so. Just wanted you to know." Chuck turned his attention to his own biscuit and coffee and they sat silently, eating.

Chuck finished his biscuit first and rose to leave. As he walked toward the kitchen's outside door he turned to Josiah and said, "Well old man, you working today? 'Bout finished with the

24-footer you been working on? Do I need to come over and help you launch her?"

"Still working on her. Ain't got another order, so really no hurry. That boat's for the grandsons anyways, you know that. Wish I had another one to start but wood boats are about finished, I think. You going fishing today?"

"Nah, what's the point. Fuel costs more than I can get in a day and besides this time of year all them Dingbatters make it too crowded, tearing up nets and all. I'm staying inside today. Bye old man." Chuck said as the door slammed behind him.

# Chapter 14 Real Estate

The Wilkins family had been on Harkers Island for generations yet in the eyes of the natives had barely progressed to the point of being considered locals. The first Wilkins had bought a large farm on the northeast tip of the island around the turn of the twentieth century and the family had been living here ever since. His great grandson, Will, now in his fifties, had been a successful contractor, working mostly on the island building houses, but the latest economic downturn, combined with a bad gambling habit, was forcing him to sell the family land and move to the mainland. He'd been approached many times over the years about selling the land but had been resolute about holding on, until his current financial situation forced him to reconsider.

The adjacent land, now called the Dunes, had been bought by the New Bern group years before, but Will had steadfastly refused to sell at that time as his business was doing well and he truly wanted to stay on the island. He had watched as the development started, then recently fizzled and had believed at the time that he'd be unable to sell his property in the current economic crisis. When Stella Stallings had approached his wife about the land, Will believed providence had smiled on him and he might be able to sell for a reasonable sum despite the times. He was baffled as to why Stallings wanted the land, but rather than look a gift horse in the mouth, had entered negotiations in hopes of a fast closing. Of course, George Stallings' murder had put an immediate halt to the proceedings and Will was resigned to his fate on the island. He was totally shocked when a few days after the murder he'd received a call from the lawyer requesting a meeting between him and Mrs.

Stallings to discuss the land deal. He'd gladly accepted and was currently waiting on his porch for the meeting to take place.

Will heard a car crunching the gravel of his driveway and within a few seconds was able to see the black Cadillac CTS as it came slowly toward him. He saw the vehicle was occupied by the driver and two passengers but was unable to recognize any of the occupants until the car stopped just a few feet from his porch. He was surprised to see not only Hall, the lawyer, with Mrs. Stallings, but her youngest son, as well, in the back seat. He remembered the son from public zoning hearings he'd attended during the land talks. Hiding his surprise, he approached the car on the passenger side and opened the door for Mrs. Stallings to exit.

"Welcome, Stella. I'm so sorry about George. It must be a great loss for you." said Will. Turning to the son he continued, "Hello JR. My condolences to you, as well."

Mrs. Stallings responded first. "Thank you, Will. We appreciate it. George was a good man and we'll all miss him. Hope you are doing well."

Wilkins invited the three of them onto his porch and soon his wife came out and after hugging Mrs. Stallings and speaking in whispers to her, she offered iced tea which all accepted. Mrs. Wilkins returned to the house to get the tea and Hall started the conversation.

"We're here to talk about the land deal before the authorities come to visit you inquiring about the same matter. We know they're coming to see you; have you been contacted yet?"

"No, not so far."

Hall continued, "Well, it's only a matter of time and we just want to make sure we all agree on what to say to them. As you know Will, George was interested in purchasing your land next to the Dunes Village currently under construction. What you may not have known is that George was also a partner in the Dunes Property as well. We wish to keep that part of the transaction as low key as possible. George's partners weren't involved in the deal with you and, as you know, Stella was handling all this part. The property you're selling was to be only to Stella without George's involvement. We're not asking you to lie, merely to tell the authorities that you were dealing with Stella and not George, which, in fact, is the actual truth. Do you understand?"

"Sure, but why the secrecy? Ya'll doing something illegal? I don't wanna be in some crooked dealing. Got enough troubles already."

"Nothing illegal, but the purpose of this land purchase might be at odds with the New Bern partners, and they may do something rash with the property they own that could sour the deal for all of us, including you."

Wilkins considered this momentarily and then said, "All right, I suppose." Wilkins' wife returned with the tea at that point and Hall reiterated the story to her as the others remained silent and listened again. JR, Stallings' son, finally interrupted by saying, "We all agree to keep the connection to the New Bern group quiet but what about the cops? Won't they say something?"

Hall answered in a very convincing tone. "I'll take care of them with a confidentiality agreement. We've spoken to the investigators already." He then produced copies of the agreement for all present to sign. Within a few minutes this was done, and the visitors were on their way back down the gravel road heading back to New Bern.

Stella asked her lawyer, "Ted, why did JR need to come here today? What does he have to do with all this?"

Hall answered, "Actually, I wanted him here as a witness to the conversation. Stella, if your family thinks that I'm taking advantage of you then all we've worked for on this deal will be lost." Hall continued, turning to JR. "No, JR, I'll not tell you all the details at your mother's request, just trust that she is doing the right thing in all this. Please don't ask me for more details."

JR, a good son, quietly accepted what his mother's lawyer asked without argument, but his curiosity was aroused as to what this land deal was really about. With his father's death, he was shouldering the responsibility of being the Pater familias and decided that he needed to know more about this deal, even without his mother's permission.

# Chapter 15 Tucker and Susan Investigation Continues

Susan's cell rang as they approached the Winston Salem city limits and looking at the screen, she saw it was the man she'd called earlier to arrange a meeting.

She answered, saying, "Good Day, Mr. Linville, my name is Susan Brown. I'm an investigator working with the FBI. Thanks for returning my call. My partner and I," she glanced at Tucker and smiled, then continued, "are looking into some burglaries of folks associated with Harkers Island and we understand you were a victim. Correct?"

Susan heard a low hoarse voice say, "The FBI? How'd you find out about the robbery?"

"We're consultants with the FBI, working with local police as well and the Garrisons in Greensboro told us about you. We hope to visit with you for a short while and ask a few questions, if that's possible."

Linville replied, "I can't see you today but I'm free tomorrow all day. When do you want to meet? Do you have my address?"

Hearing this Susan replied, "How about nine in the morning, for breakfast? At the Cracker Barrel near the Clemmons exit on I 40?"

Linville agreed and hung up after describing his vehicle so the couple could ID him the next morning.

Tucker looked at Susan in wonder, saying, "How did you know there was a Cracker Barrel at that exit? And where will we stay tonight?"

Susan chuckled and said, "I was planning on keeping you here tonight whether or not we needed to wait to see the victim. A nice evening in the downtown Marriott, some spa time, and a wonderful meal without leaving the hotel are on my agenda for the evening. Surprise!! Perhaps we can celebrate our recent engagement. At least that was my plan."

Tucker could only stare at her, almost running off the road, and finally blurted out, "Susan, I really love you!"

"Yes, I know!" was her reply as they exited the freeway into town towards the Marriott.

After they checked into the hotel, they took a stroll downtown before dinner. The streets were dark as evening began and walking along tree-lined avenues was incredibly romantic, turning their thoughts away from investigating. As they walked on the conversation gradually turned toward their future together and, after some time, Susan broached the subject of their engagement and impending marriage.

"When do you think we should tie the knot, Tucker? There's no hurry but a girl likes to plan these things, you know? Even if it's to be a small civil ceremony, it should be special. You agree?"

Tucker was somewhat surprised by this, but after a moment's consideration he turned her to face him and said, "Any time, any place, would be great for me, whatever makes you happy? Tonight, tomorrow, here, at the courthouse, in a chapel, it really doesn't matter to me."

"With my previous record, I want this one to be special, as it will definitely be my last. Two marriages in one, my third and my last!" Susan exclaimed, laughing.

They arrived back at the hotel and went inside to the restaurant to eat. Over dinner the conversation was more subdued and primarily about the case they were working on. After dinner drinks arrived and as Tucker was finishing his Drambuie, he grasped

Susan's hand and looking into her eyes intently said, "I've never been on a cruise. How about after this case is over we take a nice long cruise to the Caribbean and get married on the ship? You game?"

Susan pulled him over the table and after a long, rather emphatic kiss, she released him and leaning back said, "Oh yes, marriage on a cruise ship sounds like the perfect way to start our lives together."

They went to their room and celebrated the decision in the way people in love do. Later, in the quiet time that followed, Susan whispered, "You know, Tucker, I'll see your whole name on the marriage license."

---

The next morning, the couple arrived at the Cracker Barrel parking lot and within minutes saw an older gentleman who looked like a farmer, bib overalls, flannel shirt, green John Deere baseball cap, the whole bit, in the described vehicle. They went to meet him and Susan called out.

"Mr. Linville?" and the man extended his hand in greeting and looking up and down at Susan, smiled and said, "Pretty good looking for a cop!"

Susan blushed and returning his smile said, "Well, as I told you, we're not cops, we're consultants."

The older man just grinned bigger and said, "OK, pretty good looking for a consultant!" and then shook Tucker's hand without saying anything.

Tucker said, "How about breakfast?" and the three of them entered the restaurant. Within minutes they were seated and over coffee Tucker began to talk.

"Mr. Linville, we understand you have some properties on Harkers Island but you live here in Winston Salem, correct?"

Linville nodded and remained silent. Tucker continued.

"You were robbed here some time ago. Can you tell us what was stolen and where it was stolen? Your home? Your office?"

Linville, still looking at Susan, said, "It was April 15 th this year that my home was broken into and cash and some old jewelry was taken. I remember the exact date because of Tax Day."

"Was there anything strange done, strange for a robbery? Anything odd?"

"Like what?" Linville asked.

Tucker then said, "Anything out of the ordinary. For example, did the thieves leave anything behind?"

"Actually, they did. They left a note about how it could happen again and how I might want to stay home more. I thought it was real nutty, to be honest. Figured they was on drugs or something. The cops took the note but found nothing to identify it. It was done on a computer and there were no fingerprints. I don't think the cops really tried too hard since it was just a burglary and they knew nothing that was stolen could be identified. They'll never catch who did it."

"Well, we're going to try. Anything else you can think of?" Susan said as their food arrived. They ate in silence for several minutes before Linville raised his head and began to smile. He was obviously deep in thought and finally said to no one in particular.

"The note had a funny phrase in it. I just remembered. The exact words the note used were "you should keep yourself to home".

Odd way of putting it. I thought it sounded almost like old English when I first read it."

Tucker, with a quizzical look, asked. "Why do you say it sounds English? Do you have English friends that sound that way?"

"No, but I watch a lot of BBC, you know, English TV. It sounded a lot like something those guys would say."

Susan remained silent but her mind was racing. She felt that the wording was familiar but couldn't quite place it. They finished the meal and after lingering over coffee she slid back in her seat and rising said, "Call us if you think of anything that might help?"

Linville lagged behind as Tucker paid the bill and they walked to the parking lot together. As Tucker opened the car door for Susan he called over his shoulder, "We'll call you."

Linville merely waved and drove off. Tucker got into the truck and he and Susan started the long trek back to the coast, both lost in thought. Hours passed in silence as Susan napped and Tucker listened to NPR on the radio, all the while pondering the meaning of the notes received by the burglary victims. It was late that evening when they arrived back at the campsite. Susan had been sleeping most of the day as Tucker drove and wanted to do some internet research but Tucker was tired and after they prepared a simple meal both went to do their own thing, Tucker to bed and Susan on the computer.

# Chapter 16 Sheriff Watson

Sheriff Watson was sitting at his massive wooden desk mulling over the Stallings murder and becoming more and more frustrated by the moment. One of the deputies stuck his head in the door and offered to get coffee and Watson just growled "No" and continued to stare at his blank computer screen in disgust. He was rapidly losing patience with the local FBI agents and their lack of results on the Stallings murder. The FBI seemed to be convinced that this was just an interrupted robbery and that the killer was long gone from the area. They'd concluded that since Stallings was involved in nothing criminal and basically had no enemies that the killers were unknown to him and therefore must be transients just passing through the area. Watson knew that almost any stranger in that area was subject to intense scrutiny and would have raised red flags he would have heard about by now. Despite his belief in the basic goodness of all the area residents, Watson had a bad vibe on this one and felt in the end everything would land a lot closer to home. He decided to talk to Jessup and request possession of all the forensic data, all financial data, and basically all the evidence that the FBI had gathered. He had concluded that Jessup had a low opinion of his local agents, as well, so anticipated no real resistance to his request. He dialed Jessup's cell which was answered almost immediately.

"Jessup"

"Agent Jessup, this is Sheriff Watson down in North Carolina. I need to talk to you. Got a minute?"

"Sure. I assume this is about your murder on the island down there, right?"

Watson responded. "Yes sir, I'm not really too happy with the direction your guys down here are going. I want to expand the investigation and need your help. Maybe you could give me all the data they have and I'll go my own way and your guys can go on with what they're doing. That way none of the effort is wasted."

Jessup was quiet for a few seconds, "You think the killer is someone local. Correct? Not just a random burglary."

"Yeah! I think George knew the killer or he wouldn't have left the house with him. We don't really know where he was killed but nothing indicates it was in the house. If it was, he must have let the killer in and then left with him. If it was a stranger, I know for a fact that the island residents would have noticed a stranger out there and told me about it. I've heard nothing about any strangers and I just got a feeling it's somebody local. I hate to think it, but I do."

"What has Tucker reported to you? He's a pretty good investigator and we both need to see what he thinks. I'll talk to him first and then I'll call you. In the meantime, I'll make sure you have everything we have. I'll send you everything. How does that sound?"

The Sheriff answered yes but then realized that Jessup had hung up as soon as he finished talking, as was his way. He turned on his computer and waited for a message from Jessup that might contain information he was lacking. As he watched the screen go through its maneuvers to open, he decided to call Tucker and arrange a meeting to discuss what he'd been doing. Perhaps with the three of them involved some progress could be made. He hoped so. His patience was wearing thin.

# Chapter 17 Island Talk

Tucker was barely awake the next morning when the telephone rang, showing the local Sheriff's office number. He answered and, as expected, it was the sheriff, sounding rather short tempered.

"Tucker, have you learned anything so far? We need to combine our information and see if we're making any progress on this thing."

Tucker, having had a realization the previous evening, answered, "I have something to do today. Can we get together tomorrow? I'm sure I'll have more to talk about then?"

Watson answered with less than enthusiasm. "OK, but I really want to talk to you two soon. I'm getting political pressure to move on this case." He was exaggerating, of course, but made the point anyway. He wanted action himself, regardless of the local politicians, who had been totally silent on the matter as far as he knew.

Tucker, after a pause, replied. "I promise we'll drop by tomorrow. I'll call to arrange a time. Good-bye."

———————————————

Tucker and Susan decided to return to the small grill on Harkers Island for breakfast and then visit with Ralph again. As they drove to the island, Tucker called ahead to make sure Ralph had time for them. Ralph asked if they could meet at the grill, first thing. The wind was blowing, as usual, causing whitecaps in the sound and rocking the small boats viciously back and forth. Tucker noted the absence of the Harkers Island style boats that were so prevalent when he visited in the past.

"Susan, you should have seen the sound years ago. Then there were mostly old wooden boats rocking out there and almost none of the ones like you see now. The place has changed. I wonder if there's any real fishermen left here."

"Looks like mostly sport fishermen and not much commercial fishing at all. It's sad, but I suppose it's progress."

When they arrived at the restaurant the lot was almost full and judging from the car types and license plates on the cars Tucker figured there were mostly locals inside. They entered and found a small booth to one side where they sat down to wait. The room, filled mostly with men, quieted down and many of the patrons turned to stare at the couple. About that time Ralph entered and sat down with them after greeting several of the men by name. He leaned over and said quietly,

"I wanted you to see what happens here every third Tuesday of the month. This is the local Gripe Group. Mostly old timers that come in to reminisce about the good old days and bitch about the Dingbatters." Pointing, he continued, "The old guy in the corner is Josiah Bell, a descendant of one of the oldest families here on the island. He kinda leads the discussion, but as I said it's mostly a gripe session. Nothing comes of it, but I thought you might want to know."

Tucker responded. "I'm glad to know about this bunch. It goes to what I wanted to talk to you about."

"Well, since I last saw you guys, I've been under the weather and keeping myself to home mostly." said Ralph.

When Tucker heard that comment his thoughts of the previous evening were clarified and he felt even surer of his conclusion. He said,

"Ralph, I think there's something going on here with these burglaries and it's possible it's tied to the Stallings murder. You remember the couples we were going to talk to about being burglarized?"

Ralph nodded.

Tucker and Susan took quite a while to tell Ralph the entire story of their trip to the mainland, interrupted only by taking time to order and eat the food when it came. By the time they reached the part about Linville and his note with its peculiar phrasing, Ralph was leaning over the table looking intently at Tucker and interrupted by saying,

"I talk that way, too. You noticed that, right?"

"That was that detail I needed to convince myself. I'm still not sure that it has anything to do with the murder, in fact most likely not, but it sure is coincidental, and you know how cops think of coincidences."

Ralph had a pained look on his face as he said, "It hurts me to think that a neighbor of mine would be involved in burglaries and arson and I just can't accept murder. I just can't!"

Susan leaned close and whispered. "Probably not murder, but someone you know is likely the arsonist. Be comforted to know that the arson was done to an empty house and no one was injured."

Ralph smiled faintly and leaned back, taking a sip of coffee and allowing it all to sink in. He didn't like the thought but reluctantly conceded the possibility.

By this time the informal meeting of the residents had broken up and most of the folks had left the restaurant, which by now was nearly empty. Only the alleged ringleader, Josiah Bell, and his two grandsons, whom Ralph had identified to Tucker, remained. Tucker, speaking quietly, asked Ralph to introduce him and Susan to the Bells. Ralph, somewhat hesitantly, agreed. The three of them rose and approached the family group.

"Hello, Josiah. Hope you are doing well. Have you a second?" asked Ralph as he shook the older man's hand and then nodded to each of the grandsons.

Josiah nodded his head in acknowledgement and looked first at Susan then to Tucker, then said, "Well, the man looks a little familiar but this young lady, I've never met. I'd remember, believe me."

Tucker grinned and said, "I'm Tucker. Used to come down here a lot and fish; stayed at the old motel here on the island. I believe we may have met then. This is my partner, Susan Brown."

"What brings you to our little island, Mr. Tucker?"

"Just Tucker, sir. We first came here on a little vacation, staying at the campground over on Emerald Isle." Tucker hesitated, thinking that the truth was best as Bell would find out anyway, he continued. "We're private investigators working with the local authorities on the Stallings murder. Can we ask you a few questions, sir?"

"Sure, just Tucker," Josiah quipped. "Don't know that I can help you much. I hardly knew the man. Well, better than that, but certainly not friends. He was a Dingbatter, you know, part time resident. Didn't live here. Still a good guy!"

Susan asked. "Do you know of anyone on the island who might resent Stallings intrusion here? We know he owned a couple of houses and was in a group that wanted to develop a large property."

Josiah looking directly at Susan said, "Well, you must have heard what the folks here was talking about this morning over breakfast. It's just a bunch of us that wish the island was back like it was in our youth. Anyone here would have some resentment toward Stallings and any other part time residents here but not enough to kill him. It's not like he was one of them big land developers that want to ruin the island. As to the group, mostly we just bitch a lot and occasionally put together a petition to try to make more historical properties here and slow the development that way. Harmless and not very effective, for the most part."

Susan nodded and glanced toward Tucker, who said,

"That's what we figured. So no one really wanted him dead? Was he involved in anything illegal that you know of? Drugs, smuggling, that kind of thing."

"From what I've heard, he was pretty much a fine fellow doing nothing bad. He actually wanted to help us on the island with some things; contributed to the local church he and his wife attended. Paid for some renovations there. Nope, I don't think he'd be doin' anything illegal. You boys heard anything like that?" he continued, turning toward his two grandsons.

The two younger men had been silent throughout this conversation, but both chimed in at the same time. "No, Pop."

One of them then said, "He was a pretty good guy. He wouldn't do nothing wrong; I don't think." The other nodded in agreement.

Tucker said. "Well, if you guys think of anything that might help us, call." and handed them a napkin he had put his cell number on. "Nice meeting you."

Tucker, Ralph, and Susan left the grill and returned to the parking lot, stopping at Tucker's pick-up where Ralph said, "You didn't mention the burglaries to them, just the murder. You think they might be involved?"

"No, not really, but they might talk to someone who is. It just seemed prudent to keep that off the table in case someone on the island is really the burglar." said Tucker. "We need to confirm the connection before we say anything else. You'll keep quiet about all this, right Ralph?"

Ralph made a move to zip his lip and nodded in agreement. He went to his own car and Tucker and Susan left the island, calling the Sheriff to confirm a meeting as they drove toward Morehead City.

Watson agreed to meet with them when they arrived, so they continued straight to the Sheriff's office for the meeting.

# Chapter 18 Watson Again

A deputy escorted them into the sheriff's office as soon as they arrived despite the fact that Watson was on the telephone with his back to the door. The deputy left and Watson, finishing his call, turned to face the couple. He had an unpleasant look on his face as he said, "When I told you I was getting pressure to move on the case, I wasn't being totally truthful. At that time there was no pressure, but the call I just had was from the county manager who's up in arms about the case. Apparently there's some land deals that might be affected by Stallings murder, as if the murder itself isn't bad enough. So now there really is pressure on this. I hope you guys have good news for me. Oh, by the way, here's your PI license number; came today. The real licenses will arrive here in a couple of days and I'll call you. Congratulations on being official pseudo cops. Oh yeah, I vouched for you, so do me proud. Jessup said you guys were good, or at least Tucker. Susan, what he said about you was that you were awful tough under pressure. Tell me sometime what he meant but for now let me catch you up on what I know. Then it's your turn."

Tucker interrupted, "This could take some time. Got any coffee?"

Watson yelled for three cups of coffee and immediately went into his description.

"Since we last talked, I've had my detective go over the SBI and FBI forensic data and we believe that Stallings was not killed at his home. Eyewitnesses put him at his house the evening before the body was discovered but no one else was there and no one saw him leave. As you know his car was in the driveway when we went there to investigate. We think someone was at the home and took him. We don't exactly know how they left but that's what we believe. With the rain after the hurricane, they could have had another vehicle there or a boat and the neighbors would likely have missed it. We think it was someone he knew since there was no indication of a struggle at the house. We also think it was not a robbery."

Tucker interrupted, "Any idea about the thirty thousand dollars?"

"Nothing. If the killer looked for the money he didn't look too hard. We had no problem finding the safe. Of course, we were in no hurry and the killer would have been. We think the killer took Stallings to Shackleford and beat him with a rough shaped object, most likely a rock, then left the body there. We couldn't find anything conclusive on the island, with the rain still going on after the hurricane. This is all theory but pretty close, I think."

The Sheriff paused for a breath and to sip his coffee. When neither Tucker nor Susan spoke he continued, "As to motive, we've found nothing in his financials, family life, business, or island activity that might make someone want to kill him. Everyone just thought he was a nice guy. In short, we're pretty stymied. No motive, no weapon, so suspects, no nothing. Now, what ya got good for me?"

Tucker looked at Susan, who took over the conversation at that point.

"Well, Sheriff Watson, we haven't got much in the way of help on the murder, but we think there may be a tie into several cases on the mainland. Tucker tells me that cops don't believe in coincidences and we've found either a big bunch of them or some cases that are tied together and probably tied to Stallings murder."

She continued with the story of their visits to the burglary and arson victims on the mainland, ending with the meeting that morning at the grill with Ralph and the Bells.

Watson leaned back in his chair and stared at the ceiling for several minutes then rocking forward he looked at Tucker and said, "OK, what makes you think these Incidents are related to the murder. Seems they are surely linked together but I don't see how this ties to Stallings."

Susan said, "All the folks involved are what they call Dingbatters, part time residents on the island. All are wealthy, much more so than the local residents. All of them, except Stallings, were warned to stay home which we take to mean stay away from the island. The first, that we know of, to be warned were the Walkers who only recently returned to the island and had their house burned while they were here. The second were the Garrisons, who were also warned but have not returned. Both these couples have vacation homes on the island. The third burglary was Linville who owns several properties here and has not yet returned to the island either. Last was Stallings who owns two houses already, has an interest in the Dunes development and was currently involved in a land purchase adjacent to the Dunes property. We think that the motive behind all these events might be to keep the part timers off the island and the warnings, not being effective, were being escalated. The murder was to stop Stallings but also a warning to other Dingbatters that this island is not for them."

Watson considered this for some time until he scratched his head and said,

"Interesting theory! It actually could be accurate but we've got absolutely nothing to connect all these cases. Of course, the notes tie the burglaries together and the phrasing could tie the notes to the island. The victims do that already. There's no real connection to the Stallings murder, though."

"I know that," said Tucker, "but Susan and I are going to consider all this as we continue the investigation. Can you contact the police in New Bern and see if there's any record of burglaries involving the Stallings, or any crime for that matter? Maybe they just didn't want to tell us. Or perhaps they were warned but not burglarized and just didn't report it. Susan can ask Stella about that."

Watson said, "I'll have someone go through the state data base and look over the past several years for any burglaries involving warning notes. We'll compare that to a list of Island residents for any matches, but I'm focusing on the Stallings murder as a separate case. You guys do what you want. I guess that's all. I'll keep in touch."

Both Tucker and Susan rose and headed toward the door. As the couple walked through the lobby, Tucker turned and called to the Sheriff, "Good luck, Sheriff, we're headed to the island to try to talk to Wilkins."

# Chapter 19 Things Heat Up

Tucker and Susan wanted to go back to the island to talk to Wilkins, the man Stallings had been in negotiations with for the property adjacent to the Dunes. Earlier they'd signed copies of the nondisclosure agreement and faxed them to Hall, who'd given them the telephone number and address for Wilkins. Susan called ahead to arrange a meeting that day and Wilkins agreed to see them later in the day. They used the time to visit the local courthouse and look at real estate records to determine how much land on Harkers Island Stallings had purchased over the years. He seemed to be the focus of all this discontent with the DIngbatters, contrary to what Josiah Bell had said. What they found was the information they already had about the homes and Dunes development was accurate and was the extent of the holdings belonging to Stallings. However, they also found that Hall, the Stallings' lawyer, owned several properties on the island. Most of the sites were zoned commercial but as yet not developed or had older structures that Hall rented to the locals for their use. Of particular interest was that Hall owned the only motel in town and the waterfront property where the current small public marina was located. Of course, this had not come up in any of their conversations with the man and they both questioned whether Mrs. Stallings was aware. No conflict laws were affected but it was a strange situation. After several hours of looking through the dusty courthouse records, the couple left and headed toward the island to meet with Wilkins as planned.

Driving on the narrow two-lane road leading to the bridge accessing Harkers Island, they passed through a long section only three feet above the low-lying marsh water during the current high tide. Glancing in the rear-view mirror Tucker saw a big white van coming up very fast behind them and moved toward the right shoulder to allow the driver more room to pass. The van moved to the left lane as if to pass but when alongside Tucker's pick-up the driver swerved sharply to the right, knocking the lighter pick-up off the road and into the water. At this the van accelerated down the highway disappearing around the next curve while the pick-up, hitting the water at speed, flipped over one complete turn and came to rest lying on its side, the passenger door submerged in the dark brackish water of the marsh.

The whole thing seemed to move in slow motion until Tucker's head struck the side window, dazing him. Time passed before he slowly became aware of his surroundings. Glancing around, he saw Susan, eyes closed, mouth slightly open, head partially underwater. He reached to the limit of the seat belt holding him suspended and lifted her head up, clear of the water entering the truck cab, allowing her to breathe. Then using the shoulder harness to support her head, he began praying he'd not been unconscious too long. He reached his cell phone, dialed 911 and when the connection was made, barely had time to cry for help before passing out, in shock.

# Chapter 20 The Hospital

Tucker awakened to find himself in a hospital room connected to an IV and monitors being stared at by Sheriff Watson who said quietly,

"Welcome back to the world, Tucker. You sure took a long time to wake up."

Tucker could barely speak but managed to mumble. "How's Susan?"

At that Watson turned and went to get the nurse on duty, leaving Tucker with a sinking feeling. Almost immediately the nurse arrived accompanied by a doctor who, leaning over Tucker's bed, said quietly.

"Mr. Tucker, Mrs. Brown is alive and in surgery right now. The prognosis is good but she's suffered some minor internal injuries. We're sure those will be fine. Our main concern is her lack of oxygen during the time she was underwater. If that time wasn't too long, she'll be fine. We won't know for a few days. You need to be prepared for her having some loss of memory, brain function, and possibly mobility but she will wake up, I assure you."

"I want to see her," Tucker whispered, as he struggled to get up. "Where is she?"

It took both the doctor and nurse to hold Tucker down, such was his determination to see Susan right away. As they held him the doctor spoke with authority.

"As I said, she's in surgery. You're in no shape to get up right now. You'll be laid up for a few days with your injuries. I've given you a sedative. When you wake up you can see her if she's ready.

The sheriff wants to talk to you now and that's OK, but just for a few minutes, alright!"

Sheriff Watson had been watching all this from the door but stepped forward now and stood beside the bed.

"What happened, Tucker? Did you fall asleep or get distracted?"

Tucker replied.

"Hell no! We were run off the road by a white van, GMC, I think. I'm positive it was intentional, the way he sped up to get beside me and then swerved into the side of my truck. His van should be dented just in front of the passenger door. I didn't get a plate."

"You said he. Did you see the driver?"

"Yes, it was a man, white, brown hair, nothing exceptional."

Watson knew Tucker's history as a cop made his description likely to be more accurate than most. Eyewitness descriptions are usually of no value but this time he believed what he heard.

"Was he alone?"

"No one was in the passenger seat. It was a work van so I couldn't see into the back." was Tucker's reply.

Watson could see that the sedative and pain medicine were beginning to affect Tucker.

"Rest now. I'll come back later, and we'll talk again. Tucker, she'll be OK."

Not really a praying man, Tucker found himself praying for Susan as he drifted off. He was out within a couple of minutes, despite his worries. It would be hours later before he realized no one knew they were going to the island that morning except the Sheriff, the people in his lobby, and Wilkins. Someone had set them up or it was the strangest of coincidences, something he did not believe in.

When Tucker woke up and opened his eyes the first thing he saw was the bald head of a large black men turned away from his bed watching the small television that hung from the wall. He was rapidly running the channel selector up and down as if willing the right show to appear.

Tucker, still feeling the effects of the sedative, asked louder than he meant to, "Who are you?"

When the man turned around Tucker recognized his friend Jessup, the FBI agent, and said, "How did you know I was here? Do you know about Susan? Is she OK?"

Jessup, with a smile on his face and in his voice, said, "She's out of surgery and the doctors say she'll likely recover fully. Sheriff Watson called me and told me about the wreck. They're pretty rigid around here, but I got permission to take you to see her when you woke up. Let's go!"

Tucker felt a burden lift from his heart as he heard those words. He, Susan, and Jessup had all met during a serial killing case that was Tucker's debut as a civilian detective and the three had become pretty close, as danger often causes. Tucker could hardly control himself as he rose from the bed and nearly fell until Jessup grabbed his arm. He looked at the big man's face and smiling said, "Helping me is becoming a habit, huh Jessup."

As they walked down the hall Tucker barely heard Jessup's warning about what they were about to see, so he was a little shocked when they walked into the ICU room where Susan was lying on the bed, tubes entering her, bags of liquid hanging all around, and a small monitor screen showing every detail of her vital signs accompanied by the constant beep keeping time with the spike on the screen. Despite all this she grinned faintly as Tucker bent over her bed and kissed her lightly on the cheek.

"Is that all I get?" Susan's hoarse voice said, "Do I look that bad, Tucker?"

Tucker quickly kissed her more firmly on the lips, avoiding the tubes, and whispered so only she could hear, "God, I was so scared. You're the most beautiful thing I've ever seen, even in a hospital gown! You're OK, that's all that matters."

Her doctor swept back the curtain and entered the area saying, "All right, Agent Jessup, I told you just a few minutes, so you need to go now. Ms. Brown is very weak and needs to rest. Move it."

He glared as the two men left the area and closed the curtain behind them. Tucker heard the doctor say, "Ms. Brown, you'll be fine, but you don't need any excitement now. You can see your visitors later after you've rested for a while. We'll have you up by tomorrow."

The doctor then came out and speaking to Tucker said, "Your physician said that you could leave tomorrow morning. He'll be off and asked me to check you out. Please take the agent to your room and do your visiting there, then be ready to check out tomorrow morning. I'll drop by for a last time around seven AM and you can leave then. Ms. Brown will need to stay a few more days before I can release her. Then she'll need bed rest for a while but will fully recover, thanks to you. The paramedics told me how they found her head suspended above the water. You saved her life. I'll see you to your room."

# Chapter 21 Jessup

When the two men entered Tucker's room, after leaving the doctor who'd escorted them, Jessup sat on the chair while Tucker reclined on the bed. Jessup began the conversation.

"Let's talk about your crash first. The sheriff said you believe that you were driven off the road intentionally. Is that true? Why do you think that?"

Tucker's answer didn't surprise the agent.

"The van came up behind me very fast and then slowed as he got beside us. I'd moved over to the right to give him room in case it was some drunk needing the whole road. After he was beside us, he matched speed and then I saw him glance over at me before he swerved into my truck. It was intentional, all right. I know it for a fact."

Jessup asked, "How well did you see the guy? Would you be able to identify him."

"White guy, brown hair, average looking. I didn't get a good look at his face. I was too busy trying to stay on the road. You know the story, it all happened so fast. God, I've heard that so many times over the years, but it's true."

"Could it have been just random?" Jessup asked, knowing what Tucker's answer would be. "Just some nut on a rampage?"

Tucker said, "You don't really believe that do you? It was something to do with the case and it was planned. Someone knew we were coming and ambushed us. Before you ask, the only people that knew we were on the way to the island that day, other than the man we were meeting were the sheriff and whoever was in the Sheriff's office lobby when we left. I hollered to the sheriff our plans as we walked out of the building. Stupid!"

"Have you and the Sheriff discussed this? Is he looking into identifying his office visitors and deputies that might have heard?"

"No," said Tucker, "I've only discussed this with you. Should we involve the sheriff in this or not? What if he's the man who set us up?"

Jessup thought for a minute before replying.

"I think we must talk to him, only him, about this. If he's not involved, he'll be defensive when he figures this out on his own. Probably already has. I'll talk to him this evening and start trying to put together a list of folks in the lobby. Maybe there's a security camera. I'm going to leave now so you can get some rest. I need you on your game as soon as possible. I'll be back tomorrow morning to pick you up around eight or so. We'll go get you a rental car and then go visit the sheriff. I'll set it up for around ten tomorrow. Get some rest and don't worry about Susan. She's fine."

As Jessup walked out, he turned and nodded to Tucker, knowing that Susan would have a bedside visitor within just a few minutes. Tucker would not stay away. As he was opening the door to the black sedan the local field office had procured for him his cell rang. Looking at the display he saw Sheriff Watson displayed and quickly answered.

"Hey, Jessup! After thinking about this wreck thing for a while I believe Tucker was set up. Can you ask him who he told about visiting the island yesterday? Someone had to know that he was coming or this doesn't make any sense."

"Sheriff, we already talked about that. Tucker said the only people that knew he was going there were you, he and Susan, and the folks in your lobby when he left. He said he yelled to you as he was leaving. They didn't tell anyone else."

"Damn, I wish we had them security cameras that the county cut from our budget. I'll have my assistant put together a list of folks there at the time. The logbook should list everyone other than our employees or folks under arrest. Deputy logs will tell us about them. It'll take some time, but we can get a pretty accurate list, I think. I sure hope it wasn't one of my guys that talked, even by mistake."

"Tucker's getting out tomorrow morning and we want to come by and chat around ten o'clock. Will you be there?"

"Yeah, I'll be here." the sheriff said. "How's Susan?" and realized he was asking a dead line. Jessup had already hung up.

## Chapter 22 To Investigate or not to Investigate

Jessup was wrong about Tucker running to Susan's side right away. Instead, Tucker had raised the back of his hospital bed to support his six-foot one inch frame in a reclining position and was seriously examining his recent life decisions. The hall outside his room was bustling with people as he looked out, wondering about their lives, the danger in them, and how they handled that danger. He considered the decision to become a PI and involving Susan in that decision. He made himself face the grim fact that Susan's involvement in his investigation could have resulted in her death. This was unacceptable to him, and he knew he must move quickly to get her safely out of the hospital and somewhere she couldn't be reached by the man who'd run them off the road. He was totally convinced that the attempt on their lives had been made as a result of their involvement in the burglaries throughout the state. He was also convinced there was a direct tie in between the burglaries and the Stallings murder. First on his agenda today was to get Susan out of reach and to a safe location. He felt OK about her as long as she was here in the hospital. There was a deputy outside her door as well as his own. He rose from his bed and headed toward the hospital wing where Susan was being kept, the deputy following close behind. He walked past the nurse's station without hesitation and headed directly toward Susan's room, nodded at the deputy sitting outside then entered to find her dozing in that medication zone between sleep and wakefulness. Her eyes were barely open, and she didn't move when he approached. He stood for a long time just looking down at her beautiful face, bruised and scratched, thinking about the last several months they'd been together.

As he was standing there, he heard a cough from behind him and turned to see the doctor he had spoken to earlier standing in the doorway.

"You really shouldn't be here, Mr. Tucker."

Automatically Tucker replied, "Just Tucker, please. I know, but I just had to come here. I really wanted to talk to you. Got a minute?"

The doctor nodded and motioned for Tucker to follow him out and down the hall. "What can I do for you? I suspect you want to know more about Mrs. Brown's status, right?"

After a brief pause Tucker blurted out, "Is she really going to recover completely? How long will she need to be hospitalized? Will she need nursing care after she leaves here?"

The doctor patiently considered these questions before beginning his response. He said, "Tucker, she will eventually recover fully but it will take some time. Physically she suffered several rather serious internal injuries that will take recovery time and mentally she underwent severe trauma which will be with her for much longer. I suspect she will relive that crash in her mind for many months to come. She told me that you two live in an RV and travel together. You should consider a lifestyle change for the immediate future, at least for several weeks. I'm sure the RV is comfortable, but she needs quiet time, not in a motor vehicle, for her mind to settle down. I suggest that you check her into an area assisted living center or something similar."

Tucker interrupted saying, "I'll take care of that today. When will she be released from the hospital?"

"If she continues to respond as she is currently, within the week. I'll know more in a couple of days."

Tucker turned back toward his sleeping beauty and sat down, grasping her hand gently and said in a whisper, "Your days as Jennifer Hart are over. What was I thinking?"

Susan stirred but did not wake.

That afternoon Tucker called a local real estate agent and rented a furnished ocean view condominium in Morehead City. He went to the hospital offices and arranged for a full-time resident nurse to come and stay at the condo for the next two months. He decided to leave the RV in place at the campground for him to use as an office and to confuse anyone trying to locate them. Satisfied with the arrangements he'd made; he fell asleep in his hospital bed and didn't wake up until the breakfast cart arrived the next morning.

As he tried to down what looked like eggs but with no flavor, Tucker considered how the day would go. He decided to forgo the rental car and have Jessup take him to a dealership to pick up a new truck. Might as well take care of that right away. He knew he and Susan would be in the area for some time, so he decided to start planning for that. After the meeting with Sheriff Watson, he would go check out the condominium and see how accurate the online photos and description by the realtor had been. By the time he had finished the so-called breakfast the doctor was there to give his final OK on checking out of the hospital. The doctor looked at his chart very briefly and then pronounced him good to go. They shook hands and Tucker was alone again.

Jessup arrived about that time and with a grin Tucker announced he was ready to go as soon as they'd visited Susan for a little while. This didn't surprise Jessup, and they wandered down the hall after telling Tucker's bodyguard deputy he could go. The deputy objected until Jessup took out his badge and assured him of Tucker's safety.

Susan was sitting up, eating her food, looking considerably better than the day before when Tucker entered the room. He stepped quickly to her side and with a flourish kissed her and touched her hair softly. She broke away after several seconds and smiling, said, "Slow down big boy, I'm not healed yet." Then pulling him down by his shirt collars she convinced him that her recovery was well under way.

Jessup looked away and chuckling under his breath he thought of his own wife and how they would have behaved in similar circumstances.

Tucker pulled away and told Susan about the condo and the nurse he'd arranged but avoided any mention of his decision regarding their careers as investigators. He knew she'd be upset and today was no time to discuss it. She could help him with research on this current case after she was feeling better, but he was adamant that her career as a PI was over. If this meant that he was back into full-time retirement, then so be it. She was more important to him than any occupation could ever be.

Susan wasn't thrilled with the arrangements he'd made, suspecting there was an ulterior motive to all this, but as she'd already talked to her doctor, it was what she'd expected to happen. She knew when she was fully recovered there would be a lively discussion about their future. That was OK.

Jessup intentionally interrupted them, suspecting he needed to, and brought the focus back to the present by saying,

"Tucker, let's go get you a vehicle. We've got work to do and this lady needs her rest. You can come back up here later during visiting hours."

Tucker started to object but Susan stopped him by insisting he go, and she'd still be here this evening. As they left, Tucker nagged the deputy to be diligent and the bored woman just nodded and returned to her book after hitching up her pistol in response.

# Chapter 23 Case Connections

After Tucker had bought his four door, four wheel drive, white F150 LE truck, he followed Jessup to the sheriff's office, parking away from the crowded end of the lot to avoid dings on his new ride. He strolled up to where the FBI agent was standing where he heard,

"Pretty nice having a millionaire girlfriend, huh!"

"Yeah, it's nice. Wait till you see the condo I rented." Tucker laughed, continuing with, "It's waterfront and has a Jacuzzi!"

They entered the office where Sheriff Watson was waiting with coffee for each of them. As they approached Watson asked, "How's that girlfriend of yours? She gonna be OK? Nasty crash you guys were in."

"She'll recover fully. We're staying here in Morehead for a while until she's recuperated, but she'll be fine."

"That's good news, I'll drink to that," the sheriff said, raising his coffee cup in a toast. Noticing his large smile and red face, Tucker couldn't help but wonder what was in the coffee cup.

They sat down around the desk and Watson started the conversation.

"Like I told you, Tucker, I had my men look into the state databases for burglaries involving notes and compare that list to island residents. The three you found were only the tip of the iceberg. We found seven other burglaries, in the last two years, involving part-time residents of Harkers Island. All involved some type of note being left warning the victims to stay home more. Same as your three, cash and untraceable jewelry stolen, no real evidence and no one at home when it happened. In fact, in all the cases the residents were staying down here when they were robbed."

Tucker interrupted. "All wealthy? Elderly?"

"Yeah, just like the three you met. We also learned that the Stallings' house was burglarized before any of the others were. About two and a half years ago. There was a handwritten note that time."

Jessup chimed in with, "I got the results back on the notes you sent me. There were matching prints on two of the notes. The other was clean. It seems that the perp was learning as he went, getting better."

Tucker said, "I get the robberies, knowing the folks weren't at home, but I can't figure the notes. What was the point? Why warn victims you might rob them again?"

"A challenge? Something to confuse us? Maybe the warning wasn't just to keep the folks at home but to keep them away from the island. Harkers is the only thing that the couples have in common other than age and wealth." said Jessup.

Watson, with a wave of his hands, added, "What's this got to do with Stallings' murder? Are we on two cases or one? OK, Stallings was the first one burglarized, but do we really think his murder is part of that or just an unrelated incident?"

Tucker said in a louder voice than he intended, "No such thing as a coincidence!!" and Jessup added, "Absolutely!"

Tucker took this opportunity to tell the pair about Lawyer Hall's property on the island. While taken alone this was nothing suspicious, all agreed that in conjunction with the rest of what was going on, it deserved more attention.

This exchange of ideas went on for several minutes as the three of them continued discussing how to proceed with this investigation.

Jessup, taking control of the discussion, summarized for the group.

"Tucker, your priority is to take care of that woman of yours. You can do whatever research you can do by phone or internet. Sheriff Watson, you need to look at the group of locals that is so against the so-called Dingbatters. Also, try to find out about the van and the man that tried to kill Tucker. I'm going back to Washington to my real job. I'll do what I can to tie all these burglaries together and get the cases reopened again by getting the SBI involved since they occurred all over the state. I'll investigate the Hall property thing also. All right, guys!"

The look on Watson's face indicated his displeasure at being managed by a federal agent but he knew what Jessup said made sense.

Tucker appeared to agree on the outside but both he and Jessup knew that as soon as Susan was relocated and stable, he'd be out trying to find the man who hurt Susan and deal with him.

# Chapter 24 Susan Recuperates

Later that day Tucker went to the condo he'd rented and was pleasantly surprised to find the real estate agent hadn't exaggerated the charm of the place. Standing on the ground level back deck staring out over the ocean, he knew that Susan would find everything satisfactory for her rehabilitation. Three bedrooms, a huge kitchen, open space living area, and three baths made it both cozy and spacious, a hard thing to accomplish. Tucker selected the bedroom adjacent to the master as the nurse's station and wrote a note to that effect, placing it on the table.

He headed back to the RV to gather what would be needed to get settled into the new apartment. This took little time as all he took was some clothes and their computer equipment. By the time Tucker arrived back at the condo the resident nurse was moving in. She was an attractive woman in her early forties with short brown hair, tied back, and a fetching smile that immediately charmed Tucker.

She introduced herself as Ms. Hill but insisted on being called Tricia, saying, "That's what my friends call me and we're gonna be friends." He decided right away that the choice made by the staffing company was correct and knew that Susan would be happy with her.

When he arrived back at the hospital Susan was sitting up in her bed looking the best she had since the crash, watching the small TV and eating some of that wonderful hospital food. She grinned broadly as he approached and held out her arms toward him. After a long kiss Tucker sat down on the chair beside the bed and told her of the events of the day, including his preparations for her recuperation. While it was obvious she wasn't thrilled, she accepted her fate with little complaint, knowing it was the best thing.

"How will you get along investigating the case without me? You can't stop helping those folks just because I'm indisposed."

Tucker didn't speak for quite some time but finally said, "I was an investigator before I met you, remember. I'll keep the faith. Don't worry!" He was careful to avoid any reference to their future as investigators. He'd lost none of his resolve to keep Susan safe from harm.

They talked about things that couples talk about until Susan's doctor entered the room and interrupted them, saying.

"I have good news for you two. Susan, your recovery is nothing short of a miracle. I'm going to release you tomorrow if Tucker here has done what we discussed earlier. Tucker, do you have things ready?"

"Oh, yeah. I have a place ready to move into and the nurse is moving in as we speak."

"Excellent, excellent! All right, I'll be by tomorrow morning to check one last time and then you two can go home. I'll leave detailed instructions for therapy and return visits with the nurses who'll be here tonight. If there are any questions, I can answer them tomorrow. See you then"

Tucker and Susan both held their breath until the doctor was gone and then almost in sync said, "Thank God!" Then they both laughed as they hugged.

Tucker was so excited that he decided to stay in the room on the truly uncomfortable side chair until morning and that's what he did, holding Susan's hand the entire time. When breakfast arrived, there were two servings on the cart. As the attendant sat them both on the side table, he looked at Tucker and winked a conspiratorial wink. Tucker smiled and reached for the coffee steaming on the tray.

Check out went smoothly until they reached the door and there stood Sheriff Watson, who'd been called by his deputy when Susan's early departure became known. Watson shook hands with Tucker, then Susan and turning back toward Tucker said, "I need to keep a deputy with her, you know! Were you trying to avoid me?"

Tucker, with a grim look on his face, said, "Sheriff, until we know who called ahead when we were heading to the island, I really don't want anyone to know where we are. Please understand, no offense, but it could have been someone in your office. I've got us a secure place and no one knows who we are there. It's OK, I assure you."

Sheriff Watson just nodded slightly and finally said, "I know it wasn't one of my men but I understand. OK! When will I see you again? We've a lot to do."

"I'll call you this afternoon. Maybe you'll have some more news by then."

"We'll conference Jessup in and talk then." said the sheriff.

Susan was happy with Tucker's choice of residences and nearly as happy with the new nurse, Tricia, who had charmed her immediately as well. Susan's objection was to having a nurse at all, not to his choice. Within minutes after they met, Tricia had Susan eating out of her hand and any resentment was gone. Susan had been in a wheelchair all morning, but the activity had tired her and by the time they'd eaten lunch she was ready for a rest. Tucker helped Tricia move her into the bed and after kissing her, she drifted off to sleep. He rose, heading toward the exit. He motioned the nurse to come closer and said in a low voice, "Nothing to be alarmed about but don't open the door for anyone.

Don't acknowledge that you're here to anyone coming to the door. The agency did tell you not to let anyone at all know where you are working, right?"

Nurse Tricia said in a confident and calm voice, "I got this job because of my background. I was in Iraq for two tours and also I'm pretty good in hand to hand." She reached into the pocket of her nurse's uniform and pulled out a small automatic 380 caliber pistol and said, "She'll be OK, Tucker. Guaranteed."

Tucker was impressed. He'd asked the agency to be secretive and obviously they had made some accurate assumptions about the situation and handled his needs exceedingly well. He immediately felt better about things than he had since the attempt on their lives. As he left the condo to go visit the sheriff, he knew that Susan's recuperation would go well; she was safe in the care of Tricia, and he would find out who did this to her.

## Chapter 25 Further Case Connections

Tucker decided that he needed to talk to the Wilkins man that he and Susan had been headed to see when the crash occurred. He was certain there was something about that property transaction that was linked to the Stallings' murder. Perhaps a talk with the current owner might shed some light on that situation. Rather than chance that Wilkins was the man who arranged the attempt on their lives and would do so again, Tucker was going to surprise him with an unannounced visit. This time the drive to the island was uneventful and soon he was pulling down the overgrown dirt path that led to the Wilkins home.

Tucker knocked on the door and within a few seconds was greeted by a man who asked, "What do you want? If you're selling anything get the hell away from here."

Tucker introduced himself quickly, "I'm Tucker and if you're Will Wilkins, we spoke a few days ago and I was coming to see you then."

"Well, you shoulda come then. Pretty rude just not coming and not calling to cancel. I ain't got time for you right now."

"I was involved in a pretty bad car crash on the way to see you and was out of commission for a few days. I'm sorry but I just couldn't call."

"Well, I'm Will and we did talk. How'd you crash? Some drunk driver or were you drunk yourself?"

Tucker decided right away that Wilkins had not been involved in the attempt on their lives and that he would just be open about the situation.

"Well, we were run off the road into the water. Pretty sure it was intentional. It might be tied to the reason I want to talk to you. Now, do you have some time?"

"Yeah," Wilkins said, "Sit down here on the porch. Want a beer?"

"No thanks, but you go ahead." Tucker waited until the man returned with his longneck beer and sat down, then proceeded with his questions.

"Mr. Wilkins, I understand you're selling some property to Stella Stallings. Is that Correct?" Without waiting for an answer Tucker continued. "Do you know why she's buying the land? What she plans to do with it?"

Wilkins answered quickly. "Don't know and don't care. I just need the money more than the land. When Stella approached my wife with the offer, I was pretty relieved. Over the years lots of folks wanted the land and I didn't need the money. With the economy the way it is now I need the money and figured no one would buy it, so it was real good for me."

"Are you leaving the island?"

"Hell, yeah! I'm a contractor and even though there's some work here, it's limited, so I need to go to the mainland to work most of the time anyways. My company's in a little cash flow difficulty and moving is not so bad. I'm not one of the old timers that hate the idea of leaving this place. To be honest, I'm kinda looking forward to it."

Tucker considered his next question and finally asked, "Do you know anyone here that might feel real strong about keeping the island the same as it's always been?"

"Not really. There's that bunch that meets Tuesdays at the grill to bitch. There might be someone that's really serious but, mostly they just complain. They don't mean no harm, most likely. The folks really affected by all this are the fishermen. You might want to talk to some of them, but I don't really think you'll find anything there either."

"Why would the fishermen be that concerned with the island property?"

"It's not the land, it's the fishing. When the Dingbatters come down here every year there's so many boats out there that the fishermen have a hard time setting nets. Nets get run into and tore up by those amateurs a lot, too. It's not all that bad but some of the fishermen get pretty pissed off sometimes. I'm just saying!"

Tucker hadn't really considered this in his investigation. He thanked Wilkins and made an exit. As he walked down the grass path toward his truck he turned and said, "Will, I'm sure your land deal will get moving again quickly. Good luck with your company."

Wilkins just nodded and smiled as he downed the rest of his beer.

Tucker now had something else in the mix to think about. Perhaps a fisherman, in his frustration, had decided to kill Stallings as a warning to the Dingbatters to stay away. What had started out with a series of burglaries as warnings might have evolved into arson and murder as the warnings were ignored. If there was any physical evidence to tie the burglaries and arson to the murder, then he could be sure, but nothing had surfaced. As he drove, his mind wandered back to the Stallings' house and the young SBI forensic agent who had been working on the case when he and Susan had arrived. Suddenly a thought occurred to him and he called Jessup. Jessup answered right away.

"Agent Jessup!"

"Andy, did you send anyone down to the Stallings' house to do a forensic check?"

"Nope, that was handled by the state folks."

Tucker hoped he did not ruffle any feathers but chanced it. "The girl that was there from the SBI was pretty young and I wonder if she might have missed something."

"Like what?"

"Well, the Stallings hadn't been there in some time until that day, and I wonder if the house was checked thoroughly for fingerprints; the entire house. If the place was to be left unoccupied, I bet Mrs. Stallings cleaned it pretty well before they closed it up. Any concentration of prints, other than the victims, might be someone that met him there that night. It's possible."

Tucker heard the irritating call-waiting tone but ignored it.

Jessup responded as an agent would, "I'm sure she was thorough but to be on the safe side I'll send a crew over there to follow up. We'll look very closely at the doorknobs, light switches, kitchen counter surfaces, areas where a visitor might be. I'll let you know. It'll happen tomorrow."

"Thanks. Make sure they look closely at the back door and at the garage door. Have your guys estimate the age of the prints, if that's possible."

"It's not really accurate, but the residual oil can help somewhat, on surfaces not exposed to the elements. I'll have them be very detailed in their report. I'll be in touch."

The phone went dead as Tucker said, "Thanks again." He headed back toward the condo to spend the rest of the day with Susan.

## Chapter 26 The Evidence Builds

Sheriff Watson entered Tucker's cell number and waited as the system beeped in response. He knew Tucker was on his phone when the call immediately went to voicemail, and he heard the voice say, "This is Tucker. Leave a message." Watson recited his short message in response. "This is Watson. I need to talk to you."

When Tucker finished the call to Jessup, he looked at his display and saw that the call he'd missed was from Watson. Without listening to the message, he called the sheriff back.

"This is Sheriff Watson."

"Tucker, returning your call. What's up?"

The sheriff first inquired about Susan, asking, "How's the little woman?"

"She's doing very well. Thanks for asking. Do you have any news?"

"We found the van that hit you. It was reported stolen from New Bern about a week or so ago. Matched the paint left in the dent to your pickup and pretty much confirmed it's the van that hit you."

"Where'd you find it?"

"Abandoned in the Wal Mart lot in Morehead City. SBI's checking for prints now and we'll know something pretty soon."

Tucker almost repeated his conversation with Jessup about the SBI forensic folks but decided that it was inappropriate. After all, this should be rather simple, a truck and not a house to be scanned. He responded. "Maybe the fool left prints we can identify. This pretty much proves the wreck was a murder attempt, in any case. Call me when you ID the driver. Anything else, Sheriff?"

"Yeah. Going through all the logs and questioning all the deputies that were in the lobby that day when you left, we think we might know who set you up for the wreck. We eliminated everyone else and was left with old Charlie Barnes. He was the only Harkers man in the office and basically the only person, other than my men, who could have done it. Can't figure why he'd even care though; maybe just a coincidence. Yeah, I know what you think about coincidences."

Tucker said. "I can think of a reason, maybe. He probably didn't know that we'd get hurt but I'll wager he told someone on the island we were on the way. With your approval, I'll go talk to him. That's good work and thanks."

Watson hesitated, then said, "I think I'll go talk to Charlie. You might not be the right person for that job. Leave that to me! Oh Yeah, what did Wilkins have to say? Did you get anything new? He's an odd one."

"Nothing really. One thing I hadn't considered though. He thought maybe a pissed off commercial fisherman might try to run off the Dingbatters because they get in the way a lot. Does that sound possible to you?"

"Well, some of them guys are pretty ornery and I wouldn't put it past them. Burglary though, not murder. They're generally a nonviolent bunch, but I'll see what I hear."

Tucker said, "Let me know." and closed his cell. He remembered his conversation with Wilkins and the meeting with Ralph at the restaurant. He'd bet that Charlie Barnes was a member of the group of peaceful complainers that seemed to be more and more involved in this case. He called Ralph and was not surprised to confirm Barnes was one of the regulars in the group and had been there the morning they'd met.

———————————————————

Jessup had dispatched a forensic team from the Wilmington office to the island as soon as he had finished his talk with Tucker. He agreed that the SBI had not taken this murder seriously and to a degree felt this was his fault. With confusing jurisdictions between the body discovery on federal land, the potential murder scene on the island, and the victim being from a different county, he should have asserted himself into the case at the outset. His hesitation was in part due to the workload but also because of his discomfort in dealing with cases in the southern states. That's why he'd involved Tucker in their previous encounter. He decided, starting now, he was going to ramrod the case and if Watson and the locals were upset, he'd just deal with it.

Having reached this conclusion, he called Watson and in no uncertain terms explained the new arrangement without trying to justify it. Watson, not a stupid man, recognized the reality of this situation and in spite of some ill-will he couldn't control, immediately took up his new role and with the enthusiasm of a politician began to do his part.

Jessup began to look into the financial and land dealings of Lawyer Hall. Without a warrant the data was a collection of public records from the counties involved and newspaper records of things involving Hall. Before computers and the internet this would have taken weeks, but his team had accumulated a huge amount of information in a matter of days. They'd organized and summarized it to a point where Jessup could almost immediately begin to see the pattern. He was only a little surprised as he ran through the data.

Hall had started to quietly acquire property on Harkers Island over thirty years ago. At first purchasing older homes as the residents died and their descendants sold the old home place and moved off the island. Property values were quite low at the time and many of the families simply left for a better life. Later, as the values began to rise and the locals started to realize what was happening, he bought more commercial properties or sites that could someday be zoned commercial. He'd taken over two boat building properties when the family had all died off giving him quite a lot of waterfront land. As the owner of an LLC that he formed, he'd purchased the local motel from the old man who ran it without anyone knowing he was now the owner. He'd leased the motel and a small convenience store nearby to an immigrant couple for a ten-year span. Records indicated that there were three years left on the lease and Jessup suspected that lease would not renew, establishing the time frame that Hall was working with.

The most intriguing data was regarding the firm that had started to build the Dunes development. After digging deep into multilevel companies, he saw that Hall in fact owned almost forty five percent of the developer's company. This meant that if he were to get what the Stallings family owned, he would be the majority owner and in control of the company and thus the property.

Jessup leaned back in his office chair, put his feet up on his old gray metal desk, and staring up at the ceiling realized that this might put a whole new light on the entire case. This could have nothing at all to do with it or it could be the key to the whole thing.

He, as well as Tucker, did not believe in coincidences and was now convinced Hall was somehow involved in both the burglaries and the murder of his client and friend, George Stallings. There were three things happening here, burglaries, murder, and attempted murder of Tucker and Susan. Jessup was sure somewhere in all this the common thread was Hall. He decided to wait until tomorrow to tell Tucker all this.

# Chapter 27 Susan's Recovering

Susan had a restless night, waking both Tucker and Tricia when she'd screamed during the night. Tucker was beside her and as he'd attempted to calm her down, Tricia had arrived with a small blue pill and helped Susan swallow it. Tucker stayed in the bed until Susan finally nodded off to sleep and then went to the living room to find Tricia there, reading a magazine.

"You can go back to bed now, Tricia. I've got it."

The nurse smiled softly and said, "Tucker, she needs rest more than anything but tomorrow you should consider taking her to a therapist. She's well enough to travel short distances and this trauma could be resolved faster if she had help."

"No. We'll give her some time before taking that step. She's a very strong woman and she'll get better once she can leave this apartment and do something."

Tricia nodded but voiced her objection, "I was hit by an IED in Iraq, and it took me months to get my focus back. I just think you could shorten her trauma with some outside help."

"I'll ask her tomorrow, but I won't insist. She'll be fine."

They both retired, each knowing the other was wrong.

---

Susan woke up, rolled over and kissed Tucker's neck while rubbing his chest and said, "Wake up, sleepy head!"

Tucker said, "All right! You're still in stitches." and kissed her on the lips. She pulled away and said, "Morning medicine mouth! What did you two give me last night? Made me sleep and kept the nightmares away."

"Tricia gave you something. She wants me to get you to a therapist. What do you think?"

Susan frowned and said louder than she meant to, "That's not happening! I've had enough of those guys in my life and won't do it again."

Tucker knew nothing about her visiting a therapist but knew enough to shut up and move on.

"Well, that's settled. What you want for breakfast?" He kissed her once again in spite of the morning breath and she just smiled and said, "I'll be well soon, big boy!"

Over eggs and that southern delicacy, cheese grits, Tucker took the opportunity to catch Susan up on the news he'd shared with Jessup the day before. Susan was particularly interested in the Lawyer Hall situation and told Tucker that she'd do some internet digging for more details. Tucker immediately let her know that the computer was off limits until she was rested, healed, and sleeping through the night. Even as he made these comments, he knew it was futile and she'd do exactly what she wanted to do once he was out of sight. Oh well, he had to try. Sometimes protecting the one you love can be tiresome. He knew she'd never agree to let him continue investigations without her involvement. Hart to Hart would not become Hart alone but would simply disappear when this case was over.

After breakfast Tucker was preparing to head over to the island to locate and talk to members of the island complaint group when his cell rang, showing Jessup's number. Tucker answered and listened silently as he was told about Jessup's decision to manage the case and then even more intently as he heard about the Hall real estate dealings. The two of them agreed the lawyer was somehow in the middle of the burglaries and the murder of Stallings despite the fact Hall was ostensibly the family friend and lawyer. Tucker thanked Jessup for stepping up on the case and assured him Susan was resting comfortably and would not be involved any more. Jessup rang off abruptly when the conversation fell quiet.

Tucker, after the phone went dead, said to Susan, "Darling, you won't need to check on Mr. Hall's property holdings. The FBI has found out a lot more than we could have."

He then relayed all Jessup had told him, watching her eyes grow larger as he mentioned the extensive involvement Hall had in the island affairs. Susan reluctantly agreed with Tucker's suggestion that she return to bed and rest for the day and went into their bedroom, yawning, still groggy from the sleeping pill Tricia had given her the evening before.

Tucker finished dressing and telling the two ladies goodbye, left heading toward the island as he'd planned earlier. He had a good feeling about the day and resolved to determine if the complainers club, as he had come to think of them, had any members who might have been driven to murder.

# Chapter 28 The Complainer Group

Tucker's best bet to identify members of the group was Ralph, so he headed toward Bob's Grocery right away. When he arrived, he found Ralph in the canned goods aisle stocking the shelves with canned corn and every kind of beans imaginable, staples of the local residents. Tucker asked Ralph to accompany him outside for a minute, not wishing this conversation to be overheard by anyone. Ralph agreed, telling the young lady at the register that he was on a smoke break, winking when he said it.

Outside Tucker cut to the chase immediately.

"Ralph, I need to know the names of the members in the group we saw at the grill the other morning. We have reason to think someone in that bunch might be involved in what's going on."

"What makes you think that? I told you those guys are harmless, just like to bitch a lot. None of them are killers, I'm sure of it."

Tucker considered Ralph for a second then said, "Ralph, I've been in this business a long time and one thing I've learned is folks can surprise you. We have some pretty good evidence that at least one of the members is involved, perhaps not intentionally, but involved none the less. I won't say who, you just have to trust me on this. I need the names of all the members."

Ralph had a distraught look on his face but finally nodded and said, "You know it's not really a club or nothing, just an informal bunch. There's no membership list."

"I know. Just tell me the names of the people you see there a lot. I promise no one will know where I got this information. It would really help."

Ralph reached into his shirt pocket took out a pad and pencil and started making a list of the men he saw regularly at the Tuesday morning group session, all the while thinking how this whole thing was getting out of hand. He trusted Tucker but being an islander, it truly bothered him to provide this information. In his heart he just didn't believe any of his friends could be a criminal. But it was murder and he had to help, regardless of what came out of it.

Seeing the name Charles Barnes on the paper confirmed to Tucker he was right, and Barnes was the man who'd set he and Susan up. He'd wait for the sheriff to talk to Barnes but in his mind, it was already confirmed. Bile rose in his throat as he thought of how this man had almost had Susan killed and it was all he could do to remain calm and wait for the rest of the names.

After Ralph finished, Tucker took the note and, thanking Ralph, left the store and started his search for these individuals. He was aware that once he started interrogating any of them, the rest would be warned, but he didn't care. He knew he was on the right track with this line and be damned if he'd stop until he knew who had set them up. First stop, Josiah Bell, but he decided to call the Sheriff first about Barnes.

Sheriff Watson answered on the second ring with, "Hello, Tucker, I was just fixin' to call you. I went to see old Charlie to see if he had made the call; you know, about you and Susan. Well, he said he did call and tell the old man, that's what he calls Josiah, to let him know you were on the way. He thought that Josiah might have his grandsons get scarce in case you was wanting to talk about some late night visits they make to the old Union cemetery. I'm pretty sure he's telling the truth. He's pretty scared of cops, me 'specially. Don't know why, though."

"Why would I care about the boys going to the graveyard? What's that got to do with anything?"

"Well, everybody knows you're working with the Stallings family, and the boys sometimes trespass to find old relics from the War of Northern Aggression to sell on E-bay. I know all about it, but old belt buckles and mini balls ain't worth my time, so I just leave it alone." said the sheriff.

"I wonder who he told we were coming. I'm on my way to talk to Josiah Bell right now. Thanks for the info. I'll let you know if I find out anything."

The sheriff responded, "All right, but keep your temper. I know you're pissed about Susan but starting a war with the locals won't help us find who tried to kill you!"

Tucker sighed into the phone and said, "I'll be good, Dad!"

———————————————————

Bell was sitting on his front porch smoking and drinking something from a pint jar that looked like iced tea when Tucker pulled in the driveway. He motioned for Tucker to come on up and when he offered a drink it was obvious he wasn't talking iced tea. Tucker declined.

"How you doing today, Mr. Bell?"

"Just call me Josiah. I'm doing well. Decided to stay to home today and take a day off. Fishing's pretty crowded out there and I got no orders for boats. Good day to sit and drink a spell," he said as he took a large pull on the jar.

Tucker asked, "Do you mind if I ask you a few questions. I won't take long. It's about the Stallings case and something that happened a few days ago."

"Nope, I don't mind. Heard you had some trouble on the road. You and the missus OK?"

"Yes. I'm back in action and Susan will be in a few weeks. She was pretty battered up and almost drowned, but she'll recover."

"Was you drinking, son?"

"No, Josiah. We were run off the road. Pretty sure someone was trying to kill us or at least scare us off the island."

Josiah looked puzzled, saying, "Why would anyone want to kill you? Have you pissed somebody off asking all these questions about the Stallings thing? Everybody I know is wanting you to find out who done it so we can all sleep better. Kinda scary to think someone around here has done murder."

It seemed obvious to Tucker that Josiah was still ignorant of the burglaries and anything tying them to Stallings murder. He decided to keep that quiet for now.

"Did Charles Barnes call you and tell you we were on the way to the island the day of the wreck? This has nothing to do with your grandsons and their E-bay thing."

After considerable time spent looking Tucker in the eye, then down at the ground, Bell answered, "Yeah. He called. What're you getting at?"

"If we were run off the road then someone knew we were coming that way. Barnes told you. It looks funny, you agree?"

"I reckon it does, but I didn't have nothing to do with you getting wrecked! Why would I do that anyways?"

Tucker thought that Josiah might be just a little too defensive, so continued with this line of questioning.

"Did you tell anyone else we were on the way."

"Hell, no! I said I ain't got nothing to do with it." Bell almost yelled.

Sensing that this would take him nowhere Tucker changed the subject. He was sure that Josiah had more to say but he needed to find out what he could about the complainer group.

"OK! OK! I believe you. We talked about the bunch that meets at the grill, remember?"

"I'm old, not senile. Of course I remember. What about'em?"

Tucker worded his next question carefully, "Who in the group is the most against the Dingbatters? Maybe not enough to kill anyone, but just unhappy."

By Josiah's reaction Tucker saw he had hit a nerve. He waited for the old man to answer, hoping to get a name.

"Hell, I reckon it's me. I'd really like to leave my grandsons a business, but it looks like I'll have nothing to leave them. Hard to fish anymore and wooden boats are too slow and too much work for all the new folks here on the island. I got as much reason to hate the Dingbatters as anybody, I guess. But I ain't done nothing to Stallings."

"Who besides you has been the most hurt by outsiders buying a lot of land here?"

Bell squinted and taking another drink said, "I believe everybody in the group sorta wishes things was back like they was but like I told you last time, we're mostly old folks and not likely to be violent. We just bitch a lot."

His last comment struck Tucker as most telling. Mostly they were old folks and unlikely to use violence or to travel long distances to perform burglaries but not everyone in the group that he had seen was old. There had been Bell's grandsons and at least three other young men in the group.

Tucker rose from the rocker and said, "I've bothered you enough today, Josiah. I'll be back in touch."

Bell stood up unsteadily and walked Tucker toward the driveway.

"See you got a new truck. It's a nice'un. Hard way to trade up though!" he said, then continued, "You might want to talk to Will Wilkins. Heard he's sorta forced into a deal to sell his land, bad economy and all. He might be angry about all that. Don't tell him I sent you, though."

Tucker nodded and said, "Thanks. I'll do that." but felt pretty sure since talking to Wilkins that he wasn't forced to sell, just taking an opportunity to make something off his land. Tucker got into his truck and headed down the drive convinced that somehow Bell was hiding something. He had nothing concrete, just a cop's gut to go by, and that gut had led him to the truth many times over the years.

Tucker called the sheriff and asked, "What do you know about the Bell grandsons other than the e-bay thing? Do either of them have criminal records? Have they given you any trouble over the years?"

"Well, the oldest one, Tom, has a juvy record. Nothing all that bad. He stole a neighbor's car when he was twelve and wrecked it in the swamp coming back to the island. Too damn small to see over the wheel and ran off the road. Disappeared into the swamp and we didn't know who did it until several days later when old Josiah brought him to the office to turn his self in. You could tell the boy had his butt kicked before he came to see us. We just made the family pay for the car and dropped the charges. Other than that, they're both pretty good boys. Get a drunk on once in a while and I just ignore the young one's age as long as they do no harm. Why?"

"Just asking. Josiah acted like he was hiding something from me and I just wondered what the boys were like."

Watson said, "Them boys is all Josiah's got. He'll cover them for most anything but not murder. Not that I think they're the killer type. I really don't. You're barking up the wrong tree there, I believe!"

"Understood. Maybe he's hiding someone else in the complainer group. You have any ideas about who is the most violent in that bunch. Bell said it was him."

The sheriff was silent for a few moments then answered, "He's the most vocal but not the most violent. That'd be Will Wilkins' wife's older brother, Carl. He's been in trouble all his life. Fights, vandalism, domestic violence till his wife left him, that kind of thing. He's one of the occasional drop-in members of the group. You might want to talk to him."

Tucker said, "Yes. Where's he live? Do you have a number for him?"

"Lives in the small squatter shack behind Will's house. I'm sure he don't have a telephone but he should be there. He's on disability from that desert war back in the nineties and he don't work much. Stays around drunk most of the time. Will would let you drop by, I'm sure. They only live together cause of a promise Will made to his wife to watch out for the family drunk."

Tucker said as he turned his truck back toward the island, "Thanks sheriff, I'm on my way there right now."

——————————————————

Wilkins led Tucker to the old shack behind his house where they could see Carl through the window laying on the bed surrounded by empty beer cans. He'd been reluctant at first to allow Tucker to visit but when confronted with the fact that if Carl was involved any protection by Wilkins would most likely sour the deal with Stallings widow, he'd agreed to introduce the pair. Wilkins was sure his worthless brother-in-law wasn't involved, if for no other reason than his laziness.

Tucker knocked on the door and the figure on the bed stirred and then yelled, "What the hell do you want this early?"

"Not early! Time to get your ass up, Carl." Wilkins yelled back. "Someone here to see you. A cop."

"I ain't done nothing. Tell him to go away."

Tucker interrupted this family debate saying, "I'm Tucker and I'm not a cop. I'm an investigator. It won't take but a few minutes. We're coming in."

When they entered, they could see why Carl was so reluctant to let a cop come into his house. There was a small metal pipe on the bedside table and a bag of green matter that everyone in the room knew was marijuana. Carl placed the baggie and pipe in the drawer on the table and introduced himself.

"I'm Carl Byrd and you're Tucker, right." Carl then turned toward the bathroom closed the door, returning in just a few minutes.

"So, what the hell do you want with me?"

Tucker, disgusted with the man, said, "I'm investigating the murder of George Stallings. Did you know him?"

"Not really. Knew of him. Hell, I never had nothing to do with the man." Byrd spat.

"I'm looking at everyone in your group of locals that had ill will toward the newcomers. You're one of the more vocal ones, I'm told."

Byrd looked at Wilkins and said, "He tell you that?"

Tucker realized he was on a touchy subject and quickly lied, "Several of the members reported you were pretty hot about the invasion of DIngbatters."

Byrd cut this all short saying, "Well, I was out of town when the hurricane hit and didn't return until after that body was found. Hell, Will, didn't you miss me?", Byrd said sarcastically, then continued, "Besides, I'm not all that concerned with them guys. Just something to do on Tuesday nights. You should look at the younger folks, not at me."

Tucker sensed that Byrd knew something and asked, "Anyone in particular? Do you know anything about the murder?"

"I'd look at them Bell boys. They're both a little wild and anxious for money. If there's a dime to be made, they're most likely in it. Was the old man robbed?"

Tucker hesitated before answering, "Maybe. Why do you say the boys might be involved? Do you know something?"

Byrd just shrugged and mumbled, "No, not really. Just know the boys would do most anything for enough money. Old Josiah thinks they're angels but trust me, they're not."

Tucker cut the conversation short by asking, "Who can confirm you were out of town during the murder?" Byrd told him and that ended the conversation.

As Tucker and Wilkins walked back toward the main house Wilkins said, "He's right about them boys you know. They're not what the old man thinks they are. They might be involved but it's hard for me to think they would murder Stallings."

"People will do a lot if there's enough money at stake. I need to find why Stallings was killed and then the murderer might be obvious. Thanks for your help, Will. I'll probably be around again before this is all over. "

Tucker walked to his truck and left, deep in thought. Tucker knew it was now time to talk to lawyer Hall about his island property and his relationship with the Stallings family. When he called to arrange a meeting, he wasn't surprised to find that the lawyer was busy all this week and the next and just had no time to meet. Tucker then called Mrs. Stallings and asked to see her, thinking she would likely have Hall there, as well.

# Chapter 29 Hall, Lawyer, Entrepreneur

The next day when Tucker arrived at the Stallings' home and saw the lawyer's car in the drive, he was not surprised his plan had worked. As he turned to enter the drive himself, he saw the door open and laughed quietly as he watched Hall hurriedly approach his car, arriving before the engine died.

Hall spoke rapidly, somewhat out of breath. "Tucker, I don't appreciate you manipulating Mrs. Stallings into arranging this meeting. I told you I was busy. What's this all about?"

"We're going to talk about your property on Harkers Island and how that affected you working with the Stallings holdings. If you'd agreed to meet with me yourself, this wouldn't have been necessary."

Hall grabbed Tucker's arm as he exited the car and almost pleaded with him, but a determined Tucker continued up the drive toward the door. He shook out of Hall's grasp and went up the walk toward the door where Mrs. Stallings was waiting with a confused look on her face.

Hall hurried up the walk, quickly stepping between Tucker and the woman, all the while smiling and saying in a voice straining to remain calm, "Stella, this is nothing, really nothing to worry about! It's just a misunderstanding between Mr. Tucker and me. Nothing for you to concern yourself about. We're going to talk out here so as not to disturb you right now. I'll be in later to catch you up."

Grabbing Tucker's arm again, Hall drew Tucker along and opened his limo door wide to let him in. Hall then followed and told the driver to close the partition. As the glass partition rose,

Hall said between clinched teeth, "Dammit man, are you trying to ruin my relations with the family? I've done nothing wrong."

As the lawyer continued to ramble, Tucker interrupted saying, "If you've done nothing wrong, why are you so upset?"

"Mrs. Stallings just wouldn't understand these dealings, that's all."

Tucker sat for a few moments waiting for Hall to calm down before starting his questions. He knew there was likely nothing illegal or even unethical about this situation, but he still felt that Hall had something to hide. Owning shares in the same project as a client might simply indicate that it was a good deal, and the lawyer had guided his client's purchase as a good investment.

"Hall, when did you start purchasing the commercial property you own there? When did the Stallings start with their own land deals there?"

Hall was aware Tucker already knew the answers to these questions and was simply verifying and trying to catch him in a lie, so his answer was simple and to the point.

"Tucker, these deals are a matter of public record. You obviously already know the name of my company that made the purchases. What do you really want to know?"

Tucker remained silent for a while then responded, "You're right. I already know the answers to these questions. But I don't know the connection between your deals and his. Tell me that."

"There was no connection. We both wanted to buy land there. When I found what I considered a good investment, I advised George to participate and then helped him with the legal side."

"You have no residence there. You mostly bought commercial sites, yet Stallings was on the residential side with all his purchases. Are there some connections there?"

Hall spoke more sharply this time, "No connection. I just don't want Stella to know about what I'm doing as it might affect her feelings about the deal she's completing. I assure you there's nothing illegal here."

"What exactly is the deal she's working on?"

Hall gave the standard answer, "You know I can't tell you. Attorney-client privilege. It's nothing bad for the island residents. I'm sure nothing that would motivate murder. That's what you're concerned with, correct?"

Tucker looked Hall directly in the eyes and said, "Were you down on the island anytime during the hurricane or shortly thereafter? During the time George Stallings was killed."

Hall almost screamed, "You think I killed George? Why would I do that? Are you out of your mind?"

Tucker just stared at the man, waiting for his answer, which came only after a length tirade by the lawyer.

"I was. A couple of times during that week. Before you ask, I was alone. Checking on my holdings. I drove down and returned the same day. Sorry, I didn't bring someone to alibi me." Hall said with a bitter voice.

Tucker considered for a moment.

"I'm just trying to eliminate you as a suspect and move on to more likely candidates. You understand that don't you? Everyone's a suspect until eliminated."

Hall, visibly nervous, said, "All right. I'm just not used to being on this end of an interrogation. Who are your suspects, other than me, obviously?"

"Well, everyone, as I said. I really can't comment, you know. The investigation has expanded with the attack on Susan and me. You were aware that we were run off the road, I assume."

Hall's face was expressionless as he said, "I heard you were in a wreck. So it was deliberate, you say? I'm so glad you're both all right. Any idea who might have done it?"

"Not really. We have prints but no one to match them to. If we find who did it, we can convict, but apparently he has no criminal record or military background."

"Well, Tucker. Unless you have more questions, I have a deposition to get to in town. Sorry I was so short but being accused of murder of an old friend has that effect on me."

Hall said nothing else, merely nodded into the rearview mirror at his driver and then waited until the limo door opened on Tucker's side. Tucker, having reached his own conclusions, felt this was a good time to leave and did so without a goodbye. He walked to his truck and headed back to Morehead City and Susan, rethinking the entire conversation he'd just completed. He was convinced that Hall had some involvement in these cases but had little idea what that involvement might be. What kind of motive would a successful lawyer have to kill one of his clients? An equally puzzling question was what motive he would have for burglary? Tucker's gut, that had guided him so well in his career as a cop, told him Hall was involved somehow, and he knew he had to follow that gut. He would have Susan talk to Stella Stallings and find out what the land deal the lawyer was handling was really all about.

When he opened the door to his condo he was startled to see Tricia standing just inside the door with her handgun held in both hands pointing at him. Louder that he intended he said, "What the hell is going on?" and slowly raised his hands over his head.

Tricia, lowering the weapon, said. "Sorry Tucker, but I'm a little jumpy. We think someone tried to break in through the patio door while we were out walking on the beach."

Tucker yelled, "Is Susan alright?" as he ran down the corridor toward the bedroom where Susan should be resting.

Tricia, following, called out, "She's fine. We're fine! Just a little scared is all!"

Tucker knelt by Susan's bed and kissed her, then waiting for his pulse to stop racing, asked both the women what had scared them.

Susan answered, "The patio furniture was all tossed around when we got back here. As if someone had tried to break in. It was probably just kids."

Tucker said, "Stay here and don't open the door for anyone!"

He walked toward the front room and went out the patio door, examining it closely for damage. He walked an entire circuit around the building and, after noticing that most of his neighbor's patio furniture was upset, concluded there was no reason to think Susan was targeted. Either some vandals had been about or the wind was the culprit. He relaxed and went back inside to announce his findings.

Later, enjoying a drink and a good laugh at their paranoia, the three of them didn't notice the man peering over the lattice fence that surrounded their patio as he stood in the shadows. After a long time, he crept back toward the ocean and walked briskly down the beach.

# Chapter 30 The Pair

When the man in the shadows met his partner later that evening, the conversation centered on the two out of town civilians and their investigation. The pair had decided earlier that the investigators needed to be dealt with, since they seemed to be watching the island residents so closely. The cops and the FBI had stayed away from the locals and weren't currently a threat. The two had argued for hours over what method to use, finally deciding to cause a wreck that would take the pair out of the game for now. With the failure of the wreck to discourage the two detectives, the partners resolved to use a more direct approach. That afternoon's simple break-in and murder had been foiled when the older partner saw that the nurse was armed and might be more than he could handle. Now, in desperation, they were considering setting fire to the condo where the PI's lived, despite the collateral damage that might occur. If they were careful, they could make this look like an accidental fire, leaving no real evidence of murder. They hadn't talked to their leader, meaning to handle the issue themselves. In any case, he probably wouldn't go along with their plan to kill the private cops. Their boss could most likely avoid trouble because of his connections, but they both knew they were dead meat if caught for any of this. The money was good, but not that good. Both wished they'd stayed out of it, but it was too late. They had to go on now, no matter what it took.

"We gotta do it, man! If these two are gone, we can fool the rest of them." the older of the two said. "We can do the same thing we did over toward Greensboro; just have to do it when both of 'em are there. I know they're there now."

"Ok, OK, but this time it's gotta look like an accident. If the cops think an apartment was set fire on purpose, they'll never stop looking for who done it."

"Don't you worry! I'll do it right this time. I'm going back there tonight. I know they don't suspect anything so far since I messed up all them porches just like I did theirs. I'll call you when I'm done."

With that, the arsonist of the pair turned and left out the side door, crossing the rickety old porch and jumping into his truck for the hour-long trip back to Morehead City. He hummed as he listened to Kelly Pickler's latest hit on the radio. He'd seen enough on the patio to know just how he could start the fire, and no one would know it was deliberate. He smiled as he drove.

His partner, remaining at the house, tried not to think about what they were about to do but think about the money they'd made and the huge amount still to be made if they could just get the nosey mainlanders off their case. He hoped the fire did the job, this time.

# Chapter 31 Jessup

Special Agent in Charge Andy Jessup mulled over the facts surrounding the Harkers Island murder and the series of burglaries that seemed to be associated. He was a conservative investigator and needed to straight line everything to see the overall picture, before he allowed himself to even think about suspects. He'd spent the last day assembling the timeline from the data that the local sheriff, his own deputies, and his friends, Tucker and Susan, had provided and concluded by adding the background information that his own staff assembled. He knew from long experience the best way to do his style linear time tracking was on paper. When finished, he'd documented everything in an email and sent it to Tucker. An analysis by two investigators was always the best way and he respected both Tucker and Susan, with their logical approaches, knowing they'd help him with his thought process. He dialed Tucker's number and waited as the phone rang several times before he heard the familiar voice say, "Hey, Jessup."

Jessup replied, "Do you and Susan have a little time this morning to talk about the case? If she's up to it?"

"Yeah, we have some time, and Susan is doing real well. I'll get her and put you on speaker." After a few moments Jessup heard the sound of Susan's voice say, "Good Morning, Agent Jessup. How are you doing?"

"Please, it's Andy and I'm doing well. How about you? Are you over the wreck yet? No more nightmares, I hope."

"I'm good. Almost back to normal, a little weak is all."

Jessup, as was his style, started abruptly.

"I'll take the lead in this discussion if that's OK. I've tried to timeline what's been going on down there to understand a motive for all this behavior. If there's a common thread maybe we can see it. First the crimes. As far as we can tell some of the non-residents started getting burglarized almost three years ago. Of course, there were some that happened some earlier but we don't think they're connected, since there were no notes left behind. The first notes were handwritten, left at the homes during the burglaries, nothing traceable taken at all. Initially the notes only said the thieves might return. Later notes warned the victims to stay home more, which I think was just a more direct way of saying stay off the island. You guys know the Burlington couple had their house burned shortly after they finally decided to go back to the island. What you don't know is that there were two other couples that had the same thing happen. We believe the same people were responsible and this was just an escalated warning to the couples. George Stallings was murdered when he returned to the island after the hurricane. There must be something different about his murder, since the killer didn't go the arson route but killed Stallings. A difference we see is that he, well actually his wife, had recently started to negotiate a land deal. We think there's a connection between the land deal and his murder, but we haven't found what it is."

Tucker interrupted, "What do you know about the land deal? Anything odd there?"

"Yes, that brings me to the motivation side of these crimes. The lawyer Hall began buying land on the island long before Stallings bought his first property there. As you know the Stallings own a residence there now but had a couple of rental houses for several years before buying a place of their own. Stallings also was a part of the group that was developing the Dunes. We haven't seen any ties between the Dunes and all this. Have either of you?"

Susan, having been silent throughout all this, commented, "I've been doing research into the properties and potential uses, zoning issues, that kind of thing. I've discovered that the land Stella is after is the only land on that part of the island that can have a new marina built. The area the Dunes developers were going to use was restricted by the EPA. I'm sure her husband knew that, but she told me they were going to build a medical clinic for the island on that land. I'm convinced she thought that was the reason they were going after it, no matter what the husband knew."

After a long pause Jessup spoke, "It would seem Stallings was a key in all this, but I still don't get who might have benefited by killing him. He was trying to do a deal that would make him and the other developers rich, why kill him? Why try to keep folks off the island with the burglaries? It makes no sense."

"Unless someone, aware of the deal, wanted a part of it." injected Tucker. "Maybe Hall wanted the whole thing instead of his part as the legal counsel? He would know about the marina thing and by helping Stallings' widow buy the land, he'd be able to influence her to use it for a marina and build the clinic somewhere else, on other property he owns. Keeping the Dingbatters off the island only ties in with the land deals if there was a much larger payout without them here. Think about it, fewer part time residents means property values won't rise, for now. A marina would be a necessity in the long run for any further development. He probably plans on buying Stallings part of the development from the family. We already know that none of them are interested in anything here. Someone wants the entire island and knows that the real estate values keep going up if more mainlanders own the land here, I'm betting it's Hall. The burglaries and the murder of his friend. I wonder if Mrs. Stallings is in on it."

Susan gasped and said, "I don't believe that! No way!"

"Tucker, you might be on to something there. It's the only thing that makes any sense at all but it does seem to be a stretch. Hall, maybe, not the widow."

"Ok. How about this? Hall starts to buy commercial land on the island as an investment. He realizes that he could do a Bald Head Island thing here, you know, a private resort. He hires someone to scare off the Dingbatters to keep the land values in check. He can't stop Stallings from getting into the Dunes development without it being obvious what's going on so he kills him so he can buy the marina and Dunes land."

Susan said, "Stallings must have known about the marina and was trying to build the clinic anyways. Why kill him now? Also Stallings was a part of the Dunes thing since the beginning. Again, why kill him now?"

"Good point, baby. Something triggered this now. If we find out what, we may be able to clarify the motive. We still need proof of all this though!"

Jessup concluded saying, "You guys work on the widow. I'll try to work with the sheriff on getting some physical evidence. Still too early for a warrant on Hall's records but corporation records are public, and I'll work on the Dunes thing. Good work, Susan. You too, Tucker!"

The speaker sounded a dial tone as Jessup hung up.

Tucker and Susan decided that she would call Stella Stallings to inquire about the pending property purchase because the widow was more comfortable talking to her. With Susan still recuperating from her injuries they decided a phone call would be good enough, neither believing that the widow was guilty of anything more sinister than being duped by Hall.

Susan had the speakerphone activated so Tucker could hear the conversation between the two women. After Mrs. Stallings answered and they made small talk for a few moments, Susan went straight to the point.

"Stella, I need to ask you a few questions about your land deal there on the island. Are you still going to buy the land from Wilkins?"

"Why, yes. My lawyer is trying to arrange a closing for next week. Why do you ask? Is there a problem?"

"Oh, no! I really want to know about the adjacent property development you and George were invested in, The Dunes. Were you aware of any issues with that land? Anything that might affect the development?"

Mrs. Stallings considered for a few minutes and then said, "Should I get Mr. Hall to answer these questions? He's more involved with what's going on there since the family agreed to sell him our interest in the development."

Realizing what she had just heard, Susan quickly backtracked, saying, "Oh, that's OK. I just wondered what the deal was all about. I was just trying to find if anyone might have had problems with Mr. Stallings buying the property adjacent to the development?"

"We kept that pretty quiet so it wouldn't cause any problems with the other investors. Nothing devious, just cautious. I don't believe anyone knew but George, Mr. Hall and our family, of course."

"Thanks, Stella, I'll call again if I have any questions. Goodbye."

———————————————

Susan saw the look on Tucker's face and with a slight grin she said, "I think the theory about Hall is good. He's definitely involved somehow. But how do we prove it?"

Tucker shook his head slowly and finally said, "I'm pretty sure he did not do the killing or the burglaries himself, so we just need to find the actual killer and turn him on Hall."

"Or her!" said Susan.

# Chapter 32 The Fire

The man dressed in black left his car several blocks away from the condominium and walking briskly in the shadows finally arrived at his goal. He crept around the back of the building and approached the apartment where he knew the two private investigators were staying. Earlier that day he'd seen the containers of deck stain and solvents stored on their patio and having been a volunteer fireman, he'd been trained about the flammability of these materials and the speed with which they both dissipated in a fire. He was sure that there'd be little residue left to cause the inspectors to think arson when this fire was finished, particularly since the flammable materials were already there... He held a paper match to use to start the fire, knowing it would disappear in the fire as well. All he had to do was overturn a can of solvent causing it to spill under the patio door and then ignite the fire. Even if there were suspicions, he was confident they'd have no evidence to prove arson.

As he lit the match and saw the small flame reflected in the sliding door, he thought about how far he and his brother had come down this criminal path. Burglary, burning an empty house, then an unplanned murder and now premeditated, cold-blooded, murder. He knew it was too late to go back and as the saying went, in for a penny, in for a pound! Rationalizing the guilt by blaming the Boss, he touched the flame to the small puddle of solvent and watched as the flame followed the liquid and grew rapidly as it hit the container and pile of rags left by the workers.

He ran back several yards, stopped and turned to watch the flames as if hypnotized. He quickly walked back to his truck and left the scene without running into any other people.

Tucker was the first to smell the flames and listened to hear if a fire alarm was sounding. Hearing nothing he hesitated and wondered if perhaps Tricia had decided to sneak a cigarette inside the condo. He quickly dismissed that idea when he noticed smoke starting to come under their bedroom door. He woke Susan and together they opened the door and headed down the corridor toward the front room. Tucker immediately realized that there was a fire blazing rapidly near the patio door and hurried Susan, coughing and wheezing, toward the front. By the time he had the multiple door locks unlatched the flames were within just a few feet. He pushed Susan through the door, then turned to find Tricia.

Susan yelled, "Don't go back in there! You'll be killed!" but Tucker ignored her pleas and made a rush down the corridor past their room and into Tricia's. He found her lying on the floor, apparently overcome by smoke and dragging her to the window in her room he quickly kicked out the glass and screen and tossed her outside as if she was a child. He then followed her through the window and dragged her limp body away to safety. He heard sirens approaching and ran around the end of the condominium building to find Susan. They both came back to where Tricia lay still and began to do CPR, attempting to revive her. After what seemed like an eternity the EMT's arrived and rising, Tucker took Susan into his arms and tried to console her, all the while continuing to say without much confidence, "She'll be OK! She'll be OK!"

Tucker and Susan stood outside the burning building and watched as the firemen got the blaze under control. After what seemed like hours the fire was contained. The firemen managed to limit damage to their condo and not allow a spread to the other units, which was in itself a miracle.

"Do you think this was arson?" Tucker asked the fire chief much later, as they stood watching the smoldering rubble.

"Unlikely. No real indication of that. Likely some bad housekeeping practices. You had a fair amount of flammable material on the patio left from the work. Wouldn't have taken much to start a fire there."

Tucker replied through clinched teeth, "There was an attempt on our lives just a week ago. You need to look real close at this fire, dammit. Tricia's in bad shape and it's my fault for having her here!"

"If it's arson, we'll know soon, Mr. Tucker. There's almost always some evidence, no matter how clever the arsonist is. I promise we'll look close. I hate an arsonist, too. Sheriff's man is on the way."

Susan, having heard the entire conversation, came over to console Tucker, saying, "It wasn't your fault, Tucker. She had a job and was doing it. How could you have known they'd do this?"

"I should've figured they'd stop at nothing to get us, and we knew they used fire in Burlington." Tucker was distraught and almost sobbed as he said this.

Susan merely held him and whispered, "We'll get them! We'll get them!"

When the Sheriff arrived, he tried to calm Tucker down but was generally unsuccessful, Tucker continuing to rant and swear he would go after Hall today. Sheriff Watson, not having been briefed by Jessup yet, was somewhat confused by this and with a quizzical look asked Susan to catch him up. She summarized the conversation with Jessup.

The sheriff nodded in understanding and told Tucker, "We'll get to the bottom of this and if it's Hall, he'll pay. I promise!"

Tucker and Susan went to the hospital to check on Tricia and were waiting there when Tucker's cell rang, showing a call from Jessup. The FBI agent said without any small talk,

"You'll do nothing to let Hall know that we suspect him, understand!"

"I was just mad; I won't mess things up. I'm calm now. Did Watson call you?"

'Yes. I'm sorry about the nurse but there's nothing we can do now, except find if this was intentional and then get the bastards who did it! You need to keep your head about you and take care of Susan. I'll figure this out."

Tucker's reply didn't surprise Jessup as he said coldly, "I'm still working the case. Harder now, but I'll handle everything right. Like I said, I'm calm now and yes, we'll get whoever did this!"

———————————————————

Fortunately, Susan's recovery had been unusually fast and she was to a point where they could return to their RV without expecting any psychological impact on her. As they drove toward the campsite where the RV was set up, she turned toward Tucker and said, "You don't believe that Hall's all alone in this, do you? Killing Stallings and doing burglary, as well?"

"No, he has help. I don't know who yet. With this fire I'm even more convinced he has help. He's not doing the dirty work himself. Maybe some hired help from the mainland, maybe a local, who knows right now?"

"Do you think he's the one trying to have us killed? I've a hard time thinking of him as a killer, especially in cold blood like that and just to keep us quiet."

Tucker pondered and then said, "Well, if he had Stallings, an old friend, killed for money, he wouldn't think twice about having us killed to protect that money. We really need some physical evidence to tie Hall or his partner to the crimes. If we had that, we could turn one on the other.

As if on cue his cell rang and as soon as he saw it was the Sheriff, he answered. Without waiting for a hello, Sheriff Watson went right into his news.

"I just got a call from the SBI. They've matched the fingerprints found on the notes to the prints found in the truck that ran you off the road. We still don't know who it is, someone without a record apparently. We can eliminate Hall as the driver or burglar, though. His bar association prints are not a match. Also, the fire marshal found evidence that the fire at your condo was arson. A matchbook cover or something like that, anyways, he's convinced it's intentional. We both know it's the same person that ran you and Susan off the road. We'll get him, whoever he is!"

Tucker exclaimed, "Have you heard anything about Tricia, the nurse?"

"Not yet, but the EMT's said that if you'd been even a couple of minutes later getting to her, she'd be dead. She'll recover, Tucker. Don't you worry."

Tucker merely grunted into the phone and saying, "Thanks." disconnected. He told Susan what he'd just heard and said, "I'll find out who's helping Hall and get both of them! I'm tired of this victim role."

## Chapter 33 Murderers and Arsonists

The lawyer part of Hall's personality went along with the innocent until proven guilty legal premise, but his logical mind knew as soon as his Sheriff's Department contact called and told him that the private investigators had been burned out, his partners were involved. Partners, he mused, what idiots. First they tried to kill the couple to keep them from finding out the facts. As if stopping those two would stop the investigation. When he'd explained that the cops would continue the investigation with or without the PI's, his partners had explained their feeble logic saying, "They're the only ones that have seen us!" His fault for involving such feeble-minded men. He was stuck for now and would play through with these two. He used his burner cell to call and leave a message for them, the preferred means of communication, so he didn't have to talk to either of them. "I know you two tried to burn out the private investigators. You missed, you morons. You need to lay low starting now and stay on the island. Talk to no one. Do nothing! I'll let you know when you're free to get back to work."

He hoped the pair would listen to him and stay quiet. With the property purchase next week he would have what he'd been after all these years and could start his "Hall's Island Resort" right away. The marina property and the Dunes would get him everything he needed. What a legacy! The largest island resort on the east coast and named for him. He'd need to dispose of the pair but doing so now would draw too much attention. That would wait for a few weeks until the Stallings investigation cooled down. He'd tried to come up with a way to have them get caught for that murder and not involve him, but he was convinced they'd talk. He'd been sorry about George, but it'd been necessary, and the pair had been the easiest way to make it happen.

Hall sat back in his large leather office chair and placing his feet on the huge cherry desk he'd bought at auction from the Tryon Palace sale. He looked up at the ceiling and visualized his resort. Initially it would occupy only fifty percent of the island but his "contacts" on the local tax and zoning board assured him that within three years the property taxes and zoning changes would force the locals to sell out and allow him to buy up the remaining land. The Marina he'd build would be private, giving him control of the island water traffic. He'd arranged for the only public marina to have an environmental impact study that would force it to close. He'd spent millions in well placed bribe money, but now it was coming to fruition; Hall's Island Resort. He really liked the sound of that.

Rocking forward in the large chair he pressed the intercom button on his desk phone and called his private secretary in, beginning one of his few remaining days as a private lawyer.

At about this same time the lawyer's pair of helpers were just waking for the day. Last night's little endeavor followed by a long celebration had exhausted them and left them with headaches and huge thirst. They were as yet unaware that their plan had turned sour and that the PI's were safe and sound, unharmed by the fire. The younger of the two grabbed their untraceable cell phone and listened to the message left that morning by the mastermind. Hearing the message he exclaimed loudly, "Shit! They escaped from the fire!" He hated the lawyer's attitude and hated even more being called a moron. Turning to his partner he said, "You missed again. Damn, can't you do anything right. Hall says we're to lay low and do nothing till he contacts us. That's probably what we should do but I'm gonna try to talk him into paying us now. We'll do what we planned and just disappear. Mexico, like we planned, right?"

The other man nodded in agreement, even though he was convinced that the lawyer would never pay them now. Not until this business was completely finished would they see all their payment and then most likely they'd see a gun rather than cash. In spite of his younger partner's beliefs, he was convinced that Hall's plan for them had more to do with a gun than with cash. He knew that if you do business with a snake you might be bitten and expected no less from the lawyer. He finally decided to speak up and said quietly, "We should just take what we've made already and go. We shouldn't have tried to kill them PI's. That asshole lawyer was right. Killing them won't change nothing."

The younger man swung his fist, hitting his partner in the face with a brutal blow, causing him to lurch back and raise his hands to protect himself.

"Why'd you do that? I'm just saying! Let's just go to Mexico now, we got enough."

"Hell no, we only got a few thousand. We'd be broke soon, even down there. We're staying till we get it all. Then we'll head out. Now shut up. I'm hungry."

Checking his watch he realized it was Tuesday and added, "Let's go to the grill. Meeting day you know."

They left and headed to meet the other islanders at the restaurant to complain about the Dingbatters some more. It was, after all, their civic duty as loyal islanders to keep the island pure, at least until they got paid and left for the last time.

The younger man called Hall as they drove the short distance to the gas station where they were to eat. Hall answered, saying, "I guess you got my message. You two are pathetic. I told you not to kill those two. Now you've got the entire police force up in arms over burning an apartment building."

"We're done with those two. You was right. Pay us and we'll be out of town right away and you'll never hear from us again. Just want our money, OK?"

Hall considered briefly then said, "Yes, let me get the cash together and I'll finish the payoff. We agreed on thirty thousand, right?"

"Well, the price has gone up. What with all the attention, we think you need to pay more. You're gonna make millions off this deal. We just want our part. That'll be a hundred thousand."

Hall was unsurprised by this turn. He'd expected no less and was prepared to proceed with the deal, in his own way. They'd never get any more of his money so the agreed upon amount was unimportant.

He lied, saying, "I'll call you when I have the cash ready. Give me a couple of days"

"Two days! That's all the time you get. If you don't call, we'll call you!"

The two brothers turned toward each other and smiled. Tom thought this was just too easy, knew they were in for a fight, but kept his mouth shut. Billy would handle the lawyer, he hoped.

# Chapter 34 More Evidence

Sheriff Watson, after hearing all about the Hall connection, was able to convince his old friend Judge McCutcheon, to issue a wiretap warrant for the office and home of the lawyer. While these were being installed, he had all the public phone records pulled and searched for anything unusual of note. With the help of the SBI and FBI teams they were able to see a pattern of calls to the Josiah Bell residence on Harkers Island that occurred about two years ago, for a brief time. These calls had ceased as quickly as they started about two weeks later. There were no legal transactions on record between the two and no real estate deals, other than with Stallings, so these calls seemed a bit out of place to the sheriff. Knowing that Tucker was anxious to get back into the heart of the case, the sheriff asked him to talk to Bell and try to see what these calls might have been all about. When he called Tucker to ask him to help, Tucker responded enthusiastically.

"Oh, yeah! I'd be glad to help with this. I'll go to the complainers meeting and then talk to the old man after that. Anyone else I should contact while I'm there?"

"No. Not for now. I'll call you if something comes up. You know that if Josiah is involved he'll deny it. If it's the boys, he'll tell them and they'll run."

"I'll ask if there's been any contact with Hall about the Dune's deal. Hall was Stallings' lawyer and had a valid reason to call folks about that deal. Don't worry, Sheriff, I'll be subtle."

Tucker was glad to be back involved in the case. He'd been afraid that the fire would spell the end of it for he and Susan, but apparently this was not the case. He rose early to head to the restaurant where he knew a murderer might be waiting. He left Susan asleep in the RV with a deputy resting in his cruiser just down the path. Sheriff Watson was determined that she have no other traumatic events while in his care.

# Chapter 35 More Case Connections

When Tucker entered the restaurant all heads turned toward him, including that of Josiah Bell. He walked slowly toward the back of the room and took a seat alone in a small booth which gave him a view of the group already gathered at the front table. He opened the newspaper lying on the table, nodded at Josiah Bell and waited for the young server holding a pot of coffee in each hand to approach.

When she asked him "Regular or decaf" he said regular without looking up and followed with, "Bring me two ham biscuits as well, thanks."

Looking around, he tried to see if anyone was looking at him too intently, with any anger or fear, any outward sign of upset, but he saw nothing to note. Just a bunch of middle age to older folks, talking rapidly, mostly aimed at each other. Then focusing on the Bell table, he saw that Josiah and the two grandsons were talking to each other more than contributing to the group discussion, almost as if not interested in the content, only in their own talk. Tucker decided to take his two biscuits that had just arrived and go over for a visit.

"Good morning Mr. Bell, boys. How's it going today?"

The old man looked up and replied, "Fine as it can be. Yourself?"

"It's a wonderful day. Can I talk to you for just a few minutes, if you're done with your meeting? Won't take long."

Josiah nodded and said to his grandsons, "Y'all go on up and put that second coat of varnish on the twenty-four footer this morning. I'll be along directly, when I finish here. What can I do you for, Mr. Tucker?" Bell said, chuckling under his breath. "Still working on that Stallings thing?"

"Well, that and trying to find out who's trying to kill me and my partner." The startled look on Bell's face indicated he was unaware of any attempt on Tucker's life. Tucker continued, "Yes, first someone tried to run us off the road and put Susan in the hospital, then tried to burn down the apartment where we were staying. You hadn't heard?"

"I don't read the paper and got no TV. No one mentioned it, either."

"We're Ok. I'll find out who did it and the law will take care of him. I just wanted to clear up something you might know about the land where the Dune's is being built. Is that ok?"

"Don't know much, but I'll help you if I can."

Tucker worded his question carefully. "Did you get involved with George Stallings' lawyer, Hall, while the group was trying to buy the land? This would have been a couple of years ago."

Josiah Bell's eyebrows peaked as he remembered back, finally answering, "Not me. My grandsons talked to him some when he found out they was looking for old stuff from the union cemetery to sell. They talked a few times on the phone to him, that's all that I know of."

The conversation went on for a few minutes as they both continued to eat their ham biscuits, finally ending when Tucker said, "Well Josiah, thanks for the time. I'll be in touch if I need anything else."

Bell, looking up, said, "Hope you find out who's behind all this. Looks bad for the island if it's one of us."

Tucker thought to himself, as he headed back to where Susan was waiting, Bell is innocent but Tucker remembered what Carl

Byrd and Wilkins had said. If they'd been accurate, then one of those grandsons of his was likely the one that tried to kill him and Susan. That being the case, Tucker vowed to get him and see him rot in jail or better still try to resist arrest and get killed in the process. He just needed to find out how Hall and the boy got involved, how that connection was made. It was a good bet that the older of the two was the culprit with his juvenile record. With this thought Tucker realized that there were prints from the letters and the vehicle. There would be a record of the older grandson's prints in his juvenile record if they could get a judge to open the file. Tucker started to hum as he called Sheriff Watson for his assistance.

The sheriff was finishing his second donut, a crème filled wonder, when his deputy called over the intercom, "It's that private dick on the phone. Says it's important. You in?"

"Yeah, which line?"

Sheriff Watson then pressed the button on the only line blinking and said, "How's it hanging, Tucker? Old Bell confess to the murder?"

"No, I'm sure he's not involved but I'd like you to check the prints from the truck against that oldest grandson of his, the one with the juvenile record."

"Kinda hard to get juvie records opened. What makes you think we need to do that? What did old Bell tell you?"

Tucker replied, "He said that Hall had called the boys several times when the Dunes bunch was buying the land to check out what they were doing, selling artifacts off the cemetery. Maybe that's when the two of them connected. If we can pin the wreck on the grandson, we can clear that up at least. I'm betting one of them, the boy or Hall, is responsible for Stallings murder and will give the other up."

"If Tom's in on this, the younger one is too. Tom's too feeble minded to do anything without Billy's lead. I'll see if the judge who gave me the warrant on Hall will let us check the prints. I'll call him and let you know. How's that pretty lady doing? My deputy said she's out and about this morning, on the beach. He's staying close."

"She's doing great. Probably should have brought her to the RV right from the hospital, she's real comfortable there, it's been her home for a couple of years."

"Good news! I'll call you."

Within four hours, as Tucker and Susan were sitting outside their motorhome with the deputy on duty having lunch, the sheriff called to confirm that the prints on the truck that ran them off the road and the prints found on the two notes in the burglaries matched those of Tom Bell. Sheriff Watson had already issued a warrant for the older grandson and had deputies on the way to the island to pick him up for attempted murder and arson.

# Chapter 36 The Meeting

Billy Bell had called Hall immediately after talking to Josiah about his conversation with Tucker. He realized that the end was near, and he and Tom needed to head south without delay or risk being arrested for arson and murder. His conversation with Hall was short and to the point.

"We need the money right now. The cops are closing in and we need to skip today. If we get caught, I don't know what Tom might tell them, so we need the money RIGHT NOW!"

Hall, as he had no intention of paying the two morons for their help, lied, "Come over to New Bern. Let's meet at the campground on 17 just east of town. I'll be in my Escalade, the white one. Meet you there at two with the cash. You can leave from there to wherever you're heading."

"You better be there!" barked Billy Bell, knowing the sort of man he was dealing with.

The two brothers left the workshop where they'd been painting the boat and going across the street to their home, hurriedly gathered what little they needed to take and could get out of the house without making the old man suspicious. They threw everything into Tom's old pickup and headed off the island for the last time.

Tom screamed, "Mexico, here we come!"

"First, the money, then Mexico," Billy cautioned. "Hall's a snake and we need to be careful or he'll cheat us. After this meeting, Mexico, it is. We'll just boost us another car and head that way. "

They celebrated all the way to New Bern, turning into the campground entrance and immediately seeing a big white Caddy sitting there idling. Billy's cell rang and Hall's voice said, "Follow me; too obvious here so let's go down the road a little ways."

The Caddy left, turning left out of the lot and heading down the two-lane road toward the inlet. After ten minutes or so the big white SUV turned down a narrow unpaved side road and stopped where the road widened. Billy, suspicious, took out his small three eighty pistol and walked slowly up to the SUV. The dark tinted window started down and startled, Billy said, "Who the hell are you? Where's Hall?"

The silenced nine-millimeter made almost no noise as it discharged into Billy's brain, killing him instantly. The SUV door opened, and the driver walked hurriedly back to the pickup, jerked the door open and put two slugs into Tom's chest before he had time to react.

Within minutes the driver had removed the license plates he'd stolen earlier that day and put the originals back on the SUV. He tossed the stolen plates into the ditch as soon as he got back onto Highway 17. He called Hall and reported the problem was solved.

# Chapter 37 Susan

Waking early the next morning, Susan realized she'd had just about enough of waiting at the apartment and now at the motorhome for Tucker. After all, she'd been the one to tell Stella that they'd find out who killed her husband. Weeks later and still no word on that and two attempts on their lives, she was ready to get back involved. Her psychological issues had disappeared when they found out who caused their wreck and the fire. They'd sent the deputy away the last evening and with him had gone the feeling of being a victim, waiting to be killed.

When Tucker came into the front room of the RV, Susan was sitting inside at the dinette table, computer activated, researching land transfers involving the island. Tucker entered the living room quietly and said, almost in a whisper, "How's your day, baby?"

Susan looked up without any expression and said, "Long and boring. I'm tired of sitting here and I'm going to get back out on the case. Don't argue, I'm better and I really need to be doing something useful."

Taken aback, Tucker nodded and hugged her from the back. He nuzzled her neck and said, "Are you sure? I'm worried about you. You've been through a lot."

Realizing she'd been a little short with him, Susan turned and rose, gave him a hug, kissed him, and said, "I'm sorry! I'm just anxious to get back to work. I love that you worry about me, but I'm a big girl. I'm perfectly well."

Susan's injuries in the wreck had kept her fragile, limiting their physical contact. Both of them forgot about that as they retreated to the bedroom, ignoring everything else in the time that followed. Later, relaxing on the bed, Tucker rolled over to face Susan and said, "Do you know how much I love you? I've only been worried about hurting you. It's so good to have you back to normal."

Susan smiled up at him and said quietly, "I do know how much you love me. It's what makes all this bearable. Tomorrow we go back to work, together. Now that we know who was trying to kill us and we'll be safe, we can try to get some evidence on Hall."

Tucker nodded, for a time forgetting his earlier thoughts of getting her out of the investigation business. That was a conversation for a later date. He leaned down and kissed her again.

It was a little later when Sheriff Watson called Tucker to tell him that the Bell boys had somehow been missed by the deputies and could not be found. Since their boat was moored at their shop, it was likely that they'd left the area, perhaps to sell some of the junk they collected.

Watson was sure no one had told them about the warrants, so he figured they'd return as soon as they were finished. He'd notified all other authorities to be on the lookout and arrest them if they were sighted so it was now just a matter of time until they were caught and turned against Hall, supplying the needed testimony to indict the lawyer for conspiracy at a minimum and possibly murder as well.

The Sheriff seemed happy with this latest turn, but Tucker was worried that the Bell boys might be gone for good, taking with them any testimony against the lawyer and leaving the Stallings case open. In his career as a detective he'd had too many accomplices disappear when the case was close to being solved.

Tucker said, "Susan's anxious to get back involved so we're gonna do a little checking around. Maybe we can come up with something else to tie Hall to all this. We'll keep in touch. Call if you get the boys."

"I'll let you know if we find out anything!"

# Chapter 38 Susan's Quest

Susan and Tucker went to have a surprise visit with Stella Stallings, hoping to get to talk to her alone without Hall around. They were still trying to determine if the woman was a dupe in all this or an active participant. Both believed she was innocent and simply wanted some confirmation. Anything implicating Hall would be a bonus in this conversation. When they pulled into her drive there was a new Mercedes sports coupe sitting there, showing temporary tags.

Tucker sighed and said, "Maybe the old bird isn't as innocent as we thought. Oh, well."

"OK, she wanted a new car. Hey, you got a new truck."

They walked around the shiny new car and up the walk to ring the doorbell but before they could press the button the door opened and a man they recognized as Stella's son stepped out, closing the door behind him.

"What do you two want? Mom's been through enough already. I really don't think she's ready to see you again."

"We just want a few minutes to talk to her about what's been going on with the investigation. We won't be long. Perhaps you can ask her to let us talk to her."

JR, the son, said, "No, I don't think that's a good thing. Please leave now!"

He was interrupted by the door opening behind him and Stella saying, "Oh, shut up JR, let them in. I'm fine. How've you two been?"

Stella, hugging the older woman, said, "You look well. Are you feeling Ok? We just want a little time to talk to you. I promise we won't be long."

"Oh, you can have all the time you want. JR's been keeping me cooped up here like a hermit. I'd love the company. Let's go into the den and have some tea. Son, please have Odessa fix some tea for us and you bring it in. You can help her fix it." Stella stared at her son as she said the last part.

The three of them sat down in the front room and Tucker began the conversation with the normal small talk to put the older woman at ease.

"Mrs. Stallings, Stella, How are you making out? I'm sure it's been difficult."

"Oh, I'm OK. I miss George but the kids are here a lot. Mr. Hall, our lawyer, has been visiting a great deal as well. He's been a real help during all this."

Taking advantage of this opening in the conversation, Susan asked, "Has Mr. Hall been helping you with the financial details. It must be a nightmare, trying to keep everything going. I know you were in the middle of some land deals."

"He's been a saint. He and JR are handling everything for me. It's been a blessing. Actually, I've never known JR to be interested in any kind of real estate things. I'm so proud of how he's stepped up."

"Mrs. Stallings, what can you tell us about the land deal you are making with the Wilkins family?" Tucker asked. "How is that going?"

"Actually, I think the deal will be finalized soon. There was some delay with my husband's passing, but it's back on track now. I guess I can tell you now that we're building a clinic on the land.

We've even decided to name it the George Stallings Memorial Clinic." She lowered her head and shuddered a bit as she said this last part, obviously overcome with emotion. "It was to be called the Harkers Island Family Clinic, but JR suggested we name it after his father, and we all agreed."

Tucker, continued, "Just to confirm, this land purchase is a private deal with you and Wilkins, and not with other investors involved, correct?"

"Oh, JR can give you the details. I gave him power of attorney, so he'd know better than I."

Just then the son returned with the tea on a large silver platter and placed it on the coffee table before the group.

"I've been helping Mom with everything since the murder." JR exclaimed, having heard the tail end of the conversation. "She's got too much on her right now. That land deal is very close to finalized. What's your interest?"

"We've some suspects on another series of crimes that might be related to Mr. Stallings' death, and we're just looking for connections to them?'

"What kind of crimes? Who are the suspects?" asked Mrs. Stallings.

"Two island boys are suspected in trying to kill Susan and I as well as some burglaries on the mainland over the last three years. We haven't found them yet and it appears they've run, but it's only a matter of time till they're caught." Tucker explained.

"Who are they?" asked JR. "Are they involved with Wilkins? Is that the connection to the land deal we're making?"

"No, it's a couple of fishermen on the island. The Bell brothers. No connection to Wilkins that we know of. We were hoping you could help us with that. The reason we think they might be involved is their attempts to kill Susan and me. That could be because we were investigating the burglaries or because of your father's murder investigation, we just don't know. It had to be one or the other, otherwise, why come after us?"

Mrs. Stallings frowned and said, "That's so horrible! I hadn't heard about it. Susan, why didn't you tell me when we talked last?"

"I didn't want you to worry. We're fine. I was shaken up but I'm fine now. The worst thing is the nurse helping me after the wreck was injured in the fire at our apartment. She's still in the hospital, recovering."

Tucker, trying to control the conversation, interrupted.

"Is your lawyer handling the Wilkins deal entirely? Mrs. Stallings, is there anything about this land that might worry you? I'm sure that Hall has done his due diligence, but are you completely comfortable with everything?"

"George taught me long ago to never let anyone, even a family friend, control a transaction. That's why I gave JR my power of attorney, you know. I trust Mr. Hall, but blood is thicker than water, they always say. Why are you so concerned? Do you think those boys are involved somehow?"

"No, we know they occasionally went on the land scavenging but that's all. Oh yes, I really like your new car, Stella. Real sporty." Tucker said, grinning as he rose from the couch.

"That's mine," said JR, "Mom wouldn't drive anything like that. Besides, her Caddy is just what she needs."

Tucker and Susan glanced at each other simultaneously, excused themselves, and walked toward the door. "Goodbye Stella. We'll be in touch." Susan exclaimed as JR opened the door for them.

On the drive back toward the RV park, Susan and Tucker talked very little, as each of them tried to connect the dots on the murder and the burglaries, having no success. Eventually Tucker broke the silence saying, "Well baby, I'm about to conclude that occasionally there are coincidences. Maybe the two cases are connected only by Harkers Island and Stallings murder had nothing to do with the burglaries or the attempts on us."

Neither spoke again, but neither believed what he had just said. There are no coincidences.

# Chapter 39 Discovery

Tucker and Susan had been at home, out of contact, for the last twenty-four hours, trying to fit together the pieces of this case but with no real success. On the second day of their seclusion, the phone rang, and Tucker saw the number of the sheriff's office appear. He answered reluctantly, and heard a voice he didn't recognize say, "Mr. Tucker, the sheriff really needs to talk to you. We've been trying to get you for a few hours. Can you talk to him now?"

"Yes. Put him on!"

The sheriff spoke in short, to the point sentences, as he relayed the news to Tucker, "We found the Bell boys. Shot, dead, on an old road near the inlet, in New Bern. Their truck's there, packed for a trip. The SBI and FBI forensic teams are headed that way. You coming?"

"Text me the co-ordinates. I'm on my way." Tucker called to Susan, asking if she wanted to accompany him to a murder scene and she immediately gathered her things and they left, traveling faster than was prudent.

"I knew those boys were never going to be found alive. Damn, I just knew it! The boys were obviously not working alone. Someone wanted them silenced. It has to be Hall. I'm convinced Hall is the mastermind of this deal. Don't know how we'll prove it though.

Tucker called Sheriff Watson.

"Sheriff, we know Hall is the brains behind all this. Can you have his whereabouts checked for the time of the murders?"

"Way ahead of you. When the ME gives me a time of death, we should be able to use the ATM and street security cameras around his office to see if he was there. If he was home, we won't have any way of checking."

"Let's hope he left something for the team to find."

In less than the normal hour to drive, Tucker and Susan arrived at the crime scene and were shocked by the number of vehicles on site. Between sheriff cars, Black SUVs which must be the FBI, SBI vans, and apparently some onlookers, Susan counted twelve vehicles and at least twenty people, most standing around, but some working. She was surprised at this display of manpower but realized that a double homicide was big news in a quiet town like New Bern.

"Tucker, do you think Hall killed them, really? He's a lawyer, wouldn't he just hire someone to do it. He must have made some connections over the years to some bad characters, even in this quiet town."

"He's the type that would tie up all the loose ends on something like this. If the boys were the only ones that knew about the plot and the murder, he'd kill them himself rather than risk involving someone else that could turn on him. He's seen enough folks turn on each other during his law career to avoid letting it happen to him."

They got out of their truck and walked toward the Sheriff, standing near his car, talking on his radio. Within just a few seconds he signed off and turned toward the pair.

"The ME says that the boys died between 24 and 36 hours ago. He's confident he can narrow that range when they get the bodies back to his lab. The Forensic boys are going over the vehicle right now for anything that might help us."

Just then they heard a voice call out. "Sheriff, we've got something!"

Tucker recognized the voice of the young forensic tech that had worked the Stallings house after that murder. He felt a moment of doubt but put that away and walked with the sheriff toward where she was kneeling near the murder victim's vehicle.

"This victim, shot while sitting in the truck, fell forward into the floorboard and must have written this with his blood under the dash before he died. It looks like the word "ball". Maybe he was trying to send a message." she said excitedly.

The sheriff, Tucker, and Susan all looked at each other and grinned.

"Hall" they said almost simultaneously!

# Chapter 40 The Lawyer Hall

The sheriff was confident with this finding he'd be able to get a warrant to search Hall's office and home. Hall was well known and well respected, but with all the circumstantial evidence piling up and this dying declaration to add to it, they needed to dig deeper into the lawyer's affairs and also interrogate the man. He knew that would be a challenge because of the skills that Hall had developed as a lawyer during his career and he would need help. Watson called Agent Jessup and told him what was going on. He was pleased when the agent volunteered to come down from Washington and lead the interview with the lawyer. Watson decided to take a deputy and go after the lawyer himself, wanting to keep this as clean as possible to avoid any issues later. After telling Tucker his plan and insisting that the two of them stay out of it, then calling his friendly judge, he and his deputy went to pick up Hall for questioning. He knew the warrants would be issued immediately and the New Bern police would execute them within hours. The police chief also sent a detective to accompany the sheriff and deputy in picking up the lawyer, to ensure everything was handled correctly. Hall was a major player in town and any deviation from the letter of the law would come back to haunt them.

When the three of them arrived at Hall's office, they went straight past the front desk and pushing open the office door entered and found Hall sitting back in his big chair, feet on the red wood desk, with a large whisky tumbler, half full, in his hand. He turned toward the sheriff with a shocked look and declared,

"What the hell are you doing barging in like this? What's this about?"

"Mr. Hall, we have a warrant to pick you up as a material witness in the Stallings Murder", the sheriff said, "The paper will be waiting for us at the police station downtown. Will you come quietly, sir?"

Hall, with a calm look on his face, stood up and smiling said, "Of course, boys. I'll help you all I can with this. You could've just called and had me meet you there."

"Well, we were in the area." the sheriff quipped, "Anyways, I never had a lawyer in my cruiser before!"

Hearing this, the lawyer began to realize the reality of his situation. Sheriff Watson thought he had something or he'd be acting quite different. "What had gone wrong?" He wondered, as they walked him toward the waiting cruiser for the long ride downtown.

By the time the lawyer was situated in an interview room, Agent Andy Jessup had arrived from Washington, landing at the regional airport located in New Bern then renting a car and driving downtown to the Police station. During his ride he had been briefed by the New Bern detective assigned to the recent murders and had talked to Sheriff Watson as well about any connections that had been established between the two Bell boys and the lawyer.

"Sheriff, those calls two years ago aren't much to go on. Hall can explain them away with no difficulty. Anything concrete to tie them together? Money exchanges, prints, DNA, anything at all?"

The sheriff hesitated before answering but finally said, "All circumstantial. Nothing concrete. We needed the boys to turn on Hall and now they're dead."

"We need to pin those two murders on Hall and the rest will come out once we break that case. Hall will be easy to deal with on

Stallings if we can somehow connect him to the murder of these two. If we can't connect him to these murders, we may lose him on everything."

Jessup and the others, except for the sheriff, were convinced that the lawyer was the mastermind of all this mayhem. The Bell boys were simply not capable of a plot this complicated and didn't stand to benefit directly, so had no motive. The Stallings murder had not seemed to be a robbery gone bad, as it had been staged to appear. Jessup, rolling all this data over in his mind, reached the same conclusions he had before these last killings. The Bell boys were the burglars and Hall was responsible for the murder of George Stallings.

"OK!" He thought out loud, "Why would Hall kill the boys unless this was all tied together? He'd hired the boys to kill Stallings. That was the obvious answer to the question. Now, how do I prove any of this? Who ordered the hits on Tucker and Susan?"

That seemed out of place for the lawyer. He was too smart to try that risky and useless act, bringing attention to the case connections.

Just then Jessup arrived at the police station and after parking in a public spot a block away, walked to the front entrance. He displayed his identification and asked to be directed to the interview room where Hall was waiting. The uniform on duty, after verifying Jessup's identity, led the agent up a flight of stairs to a wide hall where the police detective and Sheriff Watson with his deputy were watching the suspect through a dark window. Minutes later, greetings done, the police detective and Jessup entered the room in view from the corridor and sat down across from Hall at the long gray metal table that looked as if it had been there since the fifties.

Jessup started abruptly, immediately going to the heart of the matter.

"Mr. Hall, you're here to clarify the relationship between you and Tom and Billy Bell from Harkers Island. Do you know them?"

"Not really. I know who they are. What's this all about?"

"Those boys were murdered and we're trying to find the killer. Your name has come up in connection with the two of them and an illegal enterprise they were involved in. We simply want to know your relationship with the pair. Did you do business with them? Have you represented them legally?"

Hall's eyes narrowed as he considered his response. Finally he said, "I knew about them gathering artifacts from the Union Graveyard where the Dunes Development will be built. Some time ago I talked to them about stopping their trespassing. That's really the only way I knew them. Am I to assume I'm a suspect in this case?"

"Everyone's a suspect. We're talking to anyone who might have a connection to the victims." the police detective said quickly, "Do you want to call your lawyer?"

"Hell, I'm the best lawyer in eastern North Carolina." Hall said with his voice rising, "Who would I call? No, I just want to be clear. I had nothing to do with the murder of those two and frankly, I'm offended by any suspicion on your part. Let's clear this up right now. When were they killed? Since I know I'm innocent, I can alibi myself and put a stop to this nonsense."

The detective continued, taking his place in the interview, "The Medical Examiner has placed the time of death yesterday, between three and seven PM. Just to eliminate you quickly as a potential suspect so we can move on, where were you during that time?"

"Check with my office. I was there working on a real estate case until around nine last evening. Security logs will verify that. We're just about done talking. This on the advice of the best lawyer I know, as I said before."

Jessup turned and looked at the mirrored window behind him and heard a light tap. Rising, he exited the room and approached the police chief who said, almost in a whisper, "He's telling the truth. We just got word from the uniforms I left at his office earlier. Both his secretary and the building security logs confirm he was there until nine last evening."

"Damn, either he has another accomplice or we're all wrong about this whole thing! We need to let him go for now. Give me a few more minutes and then come in and tell me what you just said."

The chief nodded and Jessup re-entered the interview room.

"Ok, Mr. Hall. We're checking on your alibi right now. Should have confirmation soon. In the meantime, can you tell us about your land dealings on the island? We know that you own several commercial properties there and are just wondering how this might relate to the two boys that were killed." Jessup avoided mention of the shell companies they knew were owned by Hall and held many more properties.

Hall, knowing immediately that this had nothing to do with the murders responded cautiously, "So, you've been checking my financials. Well, I'm just a landlord for a couple of stores there. Nothing to hide. I started buying properties there long ago as an investment for my retirement. I think you'll find a lot of folks here in town have done the same thing. As I said, I'm finished talking. If you have further questions, bring an arrest warrant. Don't try this material witness crap on me again. We both know it was bogus!"

Hall rose and started toward the door just as it was opened by the detective who announced to the sheriff that the alibi was confirmed, as had been intended. Hall left the room acting smug, to emphasize they could prove nothing on him. As the detective escorted him from the police station, he saw his driver waiting in the lot for him. Walking past the waiting police cruiser, he got into his car, turned and smiled widely at the detective who returned a look of disgust. Hall waved as he was driven away.

Inside the limo, Hall's calm expression changed into a grimace, eyes blazing as he closed the partition, isolating his driver and punched his cell phone.

After several rings, a voice answered, "Hello!"

"We need to talk. Face to face. Today! I just left the police station. They were asking about the Bell boys. Come to my office this afternoon at five." Hall blurted.

"OK. Just keep calm. I'll see you then."

Hall's mind was racing as he rode back toward his office. Hardly glancing out the window, he was unaware of the passage of time, trying to figure what had gone wrong. How had the cops connected him to the dead duo? Had one of them talked to the police? Slowly it dawned on him that his panic might be misplaced. Perhaps they really wanted to know about the illegal artifacts business after all. But the FBI man had specifically asked about land deals on the island, indicating he knew something. He was convinced that his skill as a lawyer made it impossible for anyone to connect him to the shell companies that owned the majority of his holdings on the island. He focused his mind on the recent turn of events that had forced him to take on a new partner in this enterprise. That was likely where the problem was. He smiled, just a bit, and realized they'd arrived at his office. When his driver opened the door, he exited and walked toward the elevator that would take him to his office on the top floor. He knew what had to be done and resolved to do it that day. The cops might suspect something but without proof, they'd be helpless. After all, he was the best lawyer on the east coast!

# Chapter 41 Josiah Bell

Sheriff Watson, reluctant to do his duty, had asked Susan to deliver the news about the grand-sons murder to Josiah Bell. While the interrogation of the lawyer was in progress, the pair arrived at the Bell residence and walked slowly up to the front, knocking softly on the door. When Josiah answered, Susan took the lead and gently, speaking slowly, she informed the old gentleman of the murder of his two grandsons. As was to be expected, Josiah nearly collapsed in shock, only remaining upright with Tucker's help. They all sat down in the living room of the old home and soon Susan's calm tone had the old man quieted somewhat and he began the expected blame game.

"I knew them boys was getting in trouble. I just knew it! Should'a been harder on them both growing up. I shoulda called the sheriff when I knew they was spending way too much money, fishing being what it is and all. Shoulda told you two what was going on when you was here! Oh, God! I coulda stopped it all!

"Mr. Bell, Josiah, it's not your fault. They were murdered and we'll find out who did it. Right now we need to know about anything going on and anyone who might have wanted your boys dead. Help us and we'll put them away." Tucker said.

Josiah Bell, wiping his eyes with his shirt sleeve, gathered himself and facing the two investigators began to tell everything he knew.

"I noticed a couple of years ago that the boys had come into some extra money, buying little things like that big screen we have in the living room, them computer games and such. Nothing big, like a car or boat or like that, just little things. At first I just figured that they'd found some good stuff in the old graveyard and sold it on that ebay thing. The next thing I noticed was that they was leaving the island for a couple of days at a time, right regular."

Susan interrupted, "Do you happen to remember when this was going on, you know, the dates?"

"Some, cause they was holidays; seems like it happened mostly on holidays. They'd always be back right after the holiday was over. I never asked them about it, they're both adults, or were."

He stifled a moan and continued.

"Then that Hall feller called them a right smart, couple of times a week for a while, and I figured that couldn't be nothing good. Why'd he want to talk to my boys, big lawyer and all? Then it just stopped."

Tucker and Susan correctly assumed that was the time that they started using untraceable burn cell phones, but said nothing.

Bell continued, "Once, Tom come home and that old truck of theirs smelled like kerosene, you know, inside the cab where you shouldn't carry such. I asked why, and he just ignored me. We don't use kerosene here at the house. I shoulda made him tell me."

He hesitated, gathering his thoughts before speaking again, "When Charlie called me and told me about you two coming to see Wilkins and you come and asked about it, I figured them boys, probably Tom, was the one that run you off the road. I just couldn't tell you. They're my boys, you know!"

Tucker suppressed his desire to hit the old man, trying to understand how he must have felt. Susan, with less emotion, said, "We understand. It's hard to turn on relatives. I know that myself."

Tucker eyed her for a moment and knew he'd have to ask about that later.

"Well, I reckon they probably did the fire too. I'm so sorry about that. Is that other woman gonna be OK? I'm so sorry."

"She's going to recover fully, but it was close. Mr. Bell, do you think your boys killed George Stallings?" asked Susan.

"Might've, I just don't know. What with all the other stuff they did, they could've. But why would they do that? He never hurt them."

"There might have been a lot of money involved. Enough money will buy most anyone, you know!" commented Tucker, "They appeared packed to leave the area when they were killed. Any idea where they were headed?"

"You sure? They didn't say nothing to me." With that Bell leapt up and ran toward the back of the house. Tucker and Susan followed more slowly.

"You're right. They took some of their stuff, mostly clothes and them computer things they had. They was gonna leave without telling me."

"May we look around, Mr. Bell? We might learn something to help us find the killer, or know where they were headed."

Josiah Bell nodded, hoping they found something to tell him what had been going on with his grandsons, right under his nose.

Tucker, opening the nightstand drawer, exclaimed. "They were headed to Mexico, it looks like. Here's some travel brochures and maps. Bell, had they said anything to you about going to Mexico?"

"No sir, nothing at all. How could they afford a trip like that?"

"Had you seen them with a lot of cash lately? In the last few days?" asked Tucker, as he realized what had probably gone on.

When the old man said no to the money question, Tucker began, "They were leaving to meet their boss to be paid. Of course, it was a set up and instead of collecting their payment for their work, they were killed in cold blood."

Josiah stood there and shook with anger and grief before saying, "Please tell me who it was. I'll handle it, myself."

"I know how you feel, but remember, these two were killers themselves. As much as you hate to admit it, they were killers. Maybe they got what they deserved." Tucker said, without any sympathy for the old man, as he thought of Susan in the hospital, nearly dying, and Tricia there, even now. "The people who did it will be punished, but not by you!"

## Chapter 42 The Beginning of the End

Tobias Hall, Esq., lawyer to the upper crust of New Bern and surrounding area, realized that it was all beginning to unravel. That last member to his little conspiracy needed to be silenced, but with the many connections to the entire mess, it would have to appear as an accident or the house of cards would crumble. It was only a matter of time before the truth came out and Hall's dreams of a Legacy Resort would die, if his cohort was left alive. As is the case with all conspiracies, the last remaining conspirators had to have total trust that the secret would remain so or distrust destroyed everything. Hall did not have that trust, knowing the truth about the situation.

Hall contemplated how he would accomplish his goal and quickly decided that a boating accident would be the easiest thing to explain, leaving suspicions but no proof. The lawyer in him knew that without proof he could get away with the murder and leave no provable evidence of a crime. He called his partner in crime using the burner cell he had used for all calls related to his crimes.

"We need to meet. The FBI is getting close."

"Call me on your office phone, we can meet to discuss our business without arousing any suspicions." the voice said. "Then throw this cell away. Do it now!"

Hall, realizing the wisdom of the suggestion, complied. Minutes later they had arranged to meet at Hall's boathouse on the river behind his home, supposedly to take a ride toward the sound and do a little fishing. It was a logical reason to go boating on this cool sunny day and would arouse no suspicions with anyone. Lawyer and client boating together and discussing a case, a reasonable activity.

Hall knew he must leave no evidence of violence when he arranged for his partner to "fall" overboard and drown. Any suspicious marks might prove to be the undoing of this "accidental death" when the ME examined the body after recovery. His plan was simple. Push the man overboard and drive away. His story was to be that the body sank quickly, preventing a rescue. It might arouse suspicions but his status in the community would help him avoid prosecution, as well as his relationship with the City District Attorney.

Hall was on board and warming up the big diesel engines of his 42-foot Hatteras Yacht when he heard, "Ahoy, the boat."

Turning, he yelled, "Come on board. We can leave; everything's good to go." and started disconnecting the dock lines and pulling the bumpers into the boat. His guest assisted and within a few minutes they were headed out the canal and into the Neuse River, leading toward the sound. The noise of the twin diesels and the wind, forced the conversation to wait until the boat slowed to cruising speed after some minutes.

Hall left the helm on autopilot, allowing him to go down to the lower deck where the other man was waiting to hear what the lawyer had to say.

The man had prepared for this meeting by bringing along his 9-millimeter, just in case the lawyer had something other than talk planned. After his time in the war, and the murder of the two Bell boys, JR Stallings was completely comfortable with the idea of killing. After all, these three men, the Bells and the lawyer, were responsible for the death of his father. He'd be perfectly content to seek his own brand of justice if it weren't for the fact that Hall controlled the land, the island contacts, and therefore the deals that would make them both incredibly rich. He would only kill Hall now to protect himself.

Hall extended his hand toward the younger man to shake and as Stallings reached out, Hall pushed him backward, off the deck, and overboard.

Stallings grabbed for Hall's hand, but this maneuver had caught him by surprise and as he fell over the side of the moving boat he screamed, "You son of a bitch," and began to tread water. Hall waved in response and continued out toward the sound. He would give JR Stallings plenty of time to drown before calling the Coast Guard on the radio to report a man overboard.

The lawyer had never killed before and wanted no part of watching the son of his old friend thrash around and ultimately sink beneath the waves, so he pushed the throttles forward, leaving the scene as fast as he could. His thoughts went to the recent events as he sped away. He knew all this mayhem could have been avoided if the people involved had simply kept to his plan. If George had just listened to reason, everything could have worked out without anyone getting hurt, but the older Stallings had been adamant about the land purchase from Wilkins. Hall sighed and watched the horizon for other boats, looking back only one time to see JR still treading water. He wondered how long the younger man could survive in the cold water before sinking out of sight. He would travel far away from this location before calling the coast guard, knowing they would locate his boat using GPS and rush to that spot to begin the search. He stared unfocused at the greenish blue water of the sound, then thinking of his plans for Hall's Resort, he smiled and began to hum softly. It was all going to work out. The only witnesses against him were dead and he could explain everything without implicating himself. He was, after all, the best lawyer he knew!

# Chapter 43 Discovery

Tucker and Susan were concentrating intensely on the documentation of Hall's real estate dealings trying to find some way to get him indicted for a crime. All involved, the sheriff, the New Bern police, Jessup, and the couple, were convinced if they could find some evidence of a crime in all this, Hall would break under questioning and confess all, particularly if they could threaten him with the death penalty for the murder of the Bells. They knew he was the mastermind in the killing even if he didn't pull the trigger himself, so the death penalty was on the table for both him and the triggerman.

The phone rang and when he answered, Tucker heard Jessup say, "Tucker, we've got him! I had the cell phone records pulled for the burner phones that the two boys used to communicate with their boss. We've been monitoring that number continuously since the murders. The same number that placed the calls to them was also used to call a third party we've now identified as JR Stallings, just minutes before the Bells were killed. This, of course, proves nothing, but that same cell was used to call JR Stallings this morning. Just a few minutes later Stallings received a call from Hall's office number. I spoke to the New Bern DA and he's getting an arrest warrant for Hall and Stallings right now. It's flimsy, but enough to hold them for a few hours. I have officers at Hall's office now and they found out he's on his boat with a client, probably Stallings. We've got the Coast Guard searching for them and when they return to shore we'll arrest Hall and Stallings for conspiracy and see who talks first."

"JR Stallings is involved? That's hard to believe. Why would he have anything to do with the murder of his father?" Tucker exclaimed.

"Probably killed the boys for killing his father. We'll get the whole story when we get them in interrogation. The New Bern Police chief will let you participate."

Hall's boat returned to the New Bern docks with only him on board and it was evident his passenger had been dropped off somewhere. There was no evidence of foul play. Despite all the circumstantial evidence to the contrary, Hall maintained that his passenger and client, J R Stallings, had fallen overboard and sank too fast to be rescued.

# Chapter 44 Interrogation and Breakdown

The smug look on Hall's face from the previous interview was still present when Jessup and the New Bern Detective entered the room to begin questioning him in earnest. Hall's answers were elusive and vague as they questioned him about the calls made with the untraceable cell phone. He was confident they had no way to tie him to the phone because he'd had the Bell brothers buy it when they bought their own. While the phone, as well as the calls, could be connected to the brothers, with them dead there was no way to trace either back to him.

Jessup was becoming more and more frustrated with Hall's ability to stonewall the questions as the interview progressed and was near to admitting defeat when he heard a tap on the one-way mirror on the side of the room. Leaving, he was met by Tucker, Susan, and the New Bern District Attorney, all wearing big grins. When he looked through the window into the adjacent interview room he realized why. There, wrapped in a blanket, hair wet, sat a disheveled and angry looking JR Stallings.

Tucker spoke first, "The Coast Guard found him swimming in the sound. Hall tried to kill him but didn't realize that his marine training left him in such good shape. He swam for 2 hours before being picked up. He's willing to turn on Hall if we can plea bargain him down to 10 years on the killing of the brothers. He says they killed his father. That's why he did it!"

The DA nodded saying, "I'm willing to do that. Anything else you find about his crimes will be on the table though. He says he was only involved in the tail end of all this. Hall will tell us more when I charge him with three counts of attempted murder and conspiracy in George Stallings' murder. If he wants to hear it from me, I'll come in, otherwise it's on you, Agent Jessup! I've some details to work out with JR Stallings!"

Jessup couldn't suppress a smile as he entered the interview room where Hall was waiting. He pointed to the mirrored wall behind Hall and motioned for the lawyer to turn around as the light behind the mirror turned on. Hall's demeanor changed visibly as he looked into the other interview room and saw Stallings sitting there talking to the District Attorney. Hall turned to face the FBI agent, his smug smile gone, and said, "What am I offered to come clean on everything?"

"The District Attorney has enough to put you on death row for the Stallings murder, as a participant in a felony resulting in a death. You already know that. If you tell everything, we can take that off the table and I'll drop any federal charges that might come up as a result of your confession and any further investigation into the land deals. You might see daylight in 25 years."

It was obvious on the lawyer's face that he was accepting his fate, but was trying to negotiate the best deal, as the competent lawyer he was.

"Will you have the DA put me in a Federal Medium Security prison, the Carolina state prison has too many people who know me?"

"Yes, if everything you tell us is accurate." Jessup replied and then waited for the story to begin. He knew that Susan and Tucker were watching through the mirror and would hear the whole thing live, not waiting for the recorded version. He smiled at the mirror and nodded to Hall to begin his story.

"I'm not a murderer! I'm guilty of hubris most of all. Several years ago, I started buying land on Harkers Island, planning to eventually turn the entire island into a resort that I'd call Hall's Island Resort. It would put Bald Head Island to shame and be the biggest private resort island on the east coast. It was to be magnificent." Hall stopped for a breath. "Not only would I be rich, but I'd be remembered forever."

Jessup interrupted, "How did this get started?"

When Hall completed his rant, Jessup had a clear picture of an egotistical, narcissistic man who would stop at nothing to be on top, no matter who it hurt. Hall had planned the resort for years and initially had purchased commercial properties slowly, and, through shell companies and acquaintances with people like Stallings, had acquired a number of residential properties as they came on the market. Realizing he needed to accelerate the process, he made contact with the Bell brothers, whom he'd met while managing the Dunes property purchase for George Stallings, to terrorize some of the Dingbatters who owned the property he needed, by burglarizing and threatening them. He'd enlisted the help of George Stallings along the way by offering large sums of money and by guaranteeing the Resort Manager's job to his son, recently returned from Afghanistan.

Stella Stallings had upset the apple cart when she talked her friend, Wilkins' wife, into selling the property adjacent to the resort, where Stella wanted to build a clinic to help the children on the island. George had finally agreed to go through with this which became a real problem when it was discovered that the Wilkins property was the only land suitable for a large marina. Not having this land would kill Halls Island Resort before it got off the ground. Hall had told Stallings about the burglaries then, believing that would keep George in the project to avoid prosecution for crimes already committed. Hall found out later from the brothers that

Stallings had tried to bribe them to leave the area by offering thirty thousand dollars cash. It was during the meeting, just after the hurricane, that Stallings had been killed when Tom had struck him with a lead weight while on their boat heading toward Stallings house for the money. The younger brother had said Tom hit Stallings repeatedly, out of control with anger, because he'd "said I was stupid". They tossed the body overboard and went on to Stallings house but were unable to find the money. It was found later by the SBI team. When word of Stallings murder became public, Hall had confronted them and they'd admitted what had happened that night. He remained silent about this until later when he decided to eliminate the brothers.

This murder, combined with the two unplanned, unsuccessful attempts on Tucker and Susan had eventually convinced Hall that it was time to eliminate the brothers. When JR Stallings, who knew about the planned resort, was told that the brothers had killed his father, he was understandably upset and vowed revenge. Hall then arranged the meeting where JR shot them both.

Hall had completed his "confession" by saying, "I never meant to do anything but build my resort. These murders were not my fault."

Jessup considered how many times he'd heard that over the years and said," Actually, they're all your fault. If you hadn't started this thing, they'd all be alive today!"

# Epilogue

Several weeks later Tucker, along with Susan and Tricia, was sitting outside the motor home, enjoying a pleasant spring afternoon sunshine when his cell rang. He answered and listened quietly, interrupting the silence only once saying, "That's good!" When he had rang off the call, he turned toward the two women and grinning, said, "That was the District Attorney. Hall pled guilty to attempted murder and conspiracy and will be in prison for at least twenty years and at his age that's life. JR was diagnosed with PTSD and will be in a secure facility until he's released, at least several years."

Tricia and Susan looked at each other, each reliving briefly the events of the winter that put them here. Susan broke the silence saying, "That deserves a drink. Stella will be glad that JR won't go to prison."

"We can help her with her affairs and finding a new lawyer. After all, our involvement started when we decided to help her after the murder."

Tricia rose from her seat and saying goodbye, headed toward her car and out of their lives. She was fully recovered and had a new job starting the next morning, looking after an older gentleman, involving nothing more dangerous than changing a bed pan.

Susan looked up into Tucker's eyes and said, "What will we do after we help Stella find a new lawyer? Do you have any plans, my dear!"

"I've booked us on a Carnival Cruise ship to the Cayman's and Cozumel leaving in about three weeks. I've also arranged a small wedding ceremony for the first night out. The captain will perform the ceremony in the Atrium area of the ship where everyone who wants to can watch. I invited Jessup and if he's free, he's coming along. Hope that's OK, darling. I just don't want to wait anymore!"

Susan, tears in her eyes, smiled and said, "It's wonderful! I love you so much!"

"We're out of the investigation business, also. I just won't risk anything happening to the love of my life."

Susan stood and they embraced in the waning sunlight for a long time before entering the motorhome, hand in hand.

# THE END

www.ingramcontent.com/pod-product-compliance
Lightning Source LLC
LaVergne TN
LVHW050541160826
845677LV00011B/2133

* 9 7 9 8 2 2 7 8 8 4 3 9 8 *